The War in Outer Space

TOM SWIFT®
THE WAR IN OUTER SPACE
VICTOR APPLETON

WANDERER BOOKS

Published by Simon & Schuster, New York

Published by WANDERER BOOKS
A Simon & Schuster Division of
Gulf & Western Corporation
Simon & Schuster Building
1230 Avenue of the Americas
New York, New York 10020
Manufactured in the United States of America
10 9 8 7 6 5 4 3
WANDERER and colophon are trademarks
of Simon & Schuster
TOM SWIFT is a trademark of Stratemeyer Syndicate,
registered in the United States Patent and Trademark Office

Library of Congress Cataloging in Publication Data
Appleton, Victor, pseud.
The war in outer space.

(Tom Swift/Victor Appleton; no. 4)
Summary: In the first hyper-drive spacecraft,
Tom, Ben, and Anita try to make contact with an
alien race that built a probe.
[1. Science fiction]   I. Title.   II. Series:
Appleton, Victor, pseud. Tom Swift; no. 4.
PZ7.A652War   [Fic]   81-4460
    ISBN 0-671-42539-0   AACR2
        ISBN 0-671-42579-X (pbk.)

CONTENTS

Chapter One	7
Chapter Two	15
Chapter Three	27
Chapter Four	37
Chapter Five	48
Chapter Six	60
Chapter Seven	66
Chapter Eight	77
Chapter Nine	89
Chapter Ten	100
Chapter Eleven	110
Chapter Twelve	121
Chapter Thirteen	132
Chapter Fourteen	142
Chapter Fifteen	152
Chapter Sixteen	160

Chapter One

EEEEEEE!

The sudden, ear-piercing sound of the space-ship's emergency alarm jolted Tom Swift to instant alertness. If he had not been strapped into the contoured pilot's couch, he would have reacted by jumping up.

Instead he quickly scanned the control panel in front of him, seeking the cause of the alarm. Every light on the corner of the panel labeled AUTOMATIC EXTERIOR DEFENSE SUBSYSTEM began flashing red. The next instant, Tom felt his ship's engines surge forward as if they had suddenly developed a mind and will of their own.

"What's the—!" shouted Benjamin Franklin

Walking Eagle, Tom's best friend and copilot.

Without warning the vessel pitched violently to the right and both boys had to fight a sickening feeling of vertigo as the stars outside the front port appeared to rotate.

"The automatic meteor defense subsystem has just taken over!" Tom shouted above the wailing siren. "Try to get that rock on the screen," he commanded. "It must be the size of a small moon to cause the ship to react like this."

Even before the eighteen-year-old inventor had finished speaking, Ben had activated the exterior cameras and punched a set of instructions into the computer, telling it exactly where to locate the meteor. The monitors lit up with views of the space surrounding their ship, the *Exedra.*

What the two friends saw on the screen shocked them more than even the largest meteor would have. A sleek, fighter-class spaceship was heading toward them on a deliberate collision course!

Tom reacted instantly with the instincts of a born leader. "Cut that alarm and let's get that rocket off our tail," he said as he expertly maneuvered the switches and control buttons in front of him.

"It won't be easy, Tom," Ben replied, scanning his computerscreen. "The computer is no longer using the meteor defense subsystem. The *Exedra* is now being controlled by the battle computer subsystem."

"What?" Tom flicked a switch to put the printout on his viewscreen as well. "I'd momentarily forgotten we had a separate battle computer."

"We do. And it must have decided that ship out there was a threat because it was on a collision course with us," Ben suggested. "On that basis, the battle computer simply took over. After all, that's the logical thing for it to do."

Ben was a genius with computers. In fact, it was his flair for using them creatively which had first brought the two boys together. The dark-haired Cherokee Indian had shared several adventures with Tom and their mutual friend, a saucy redhead named Anita Thorwald.

For the last several months, the three young people, aided by Tom's faithful robot, Aristotle, had worked hard on rebuilding the spaceship *Exedra* at Swift Enterprises' main headquarters in Shopton, New Mexico. Originally a fighter, the ship had been converted into a luxury spaceyacht before Swift Enterprises had acquired the vessel.

On an expedition to Io, one of the moons of Jupiter, Tom, Anita, Ben, and Aristotle had discovered an alien probe sent from a distant solar system. The probe had been instructed by its people, the Skree, to seek out other forms of intelligent life who would aid them in their war with their archenemies, the Chutans.

In exchange for this assistance, the Skree promised no less than a genuine stardrive—a way to travel faster than the speed of light!

Though the probe itself had been destroyed before revealing all the details, Aristotle had managed to obtain a good quantity of the necessary technical information. Working together, Tom and Ben had finally discovered the secret.

The last few months had been spent refitting the *Exedra* with the newly built stardrive. Anita and Aristotle had gone to *New America* for some last-minute work on a few minor parts which could be made much more accurately in the zero-gravity of the space colony which orbited Earth. Tom and Ben were on their way to *New America* now to pick them up for the big test of the stardrive during which they were planning to contact the Skree and offer their assistance.

Suddenly it looked as if the test might never take place!

"It's probably been years since this ship saw any battle action—if it ever did," Tom observed.

"There's no way to tell if the laser cannons have ever been fired," Ben said thoughtfully.

"But I know they work. The problem is, I didn't reprogram the battle computer subsystem for the new stardrive. Whatever *Exedra* does now, she'll do as a result of her original programing!"

Tom looked at his friend in horror. "There's one problem with that," the blond boy said. "The programing was designed to utilize *Exedra*'s original capabilities. We've got an entirely rebuilt ship now!"

Ben nodded. "I know." He scanned the digital readouts which were pouring out rapidly from the ship's computer. "I'm trying to determine what those changes might mean to the subsystem."

A warning light flashed a red signal, indicating the mysterious ship was continuing its collision course and was drawing dangerously near.

"Well, the solid-fuel attitude engines on the outriggers have been augmented by fusion motors," Tom said. "That means this ship is now the fastest, most powerful vessel ever built by man. It's a real starship! The battle computer subsystem has all that power to draw upon."

"Exactly," the young computer technician said. "No ship I know of is capable of getting out of our way fast enough if the *Exedra* decided to take some fancy evasive maneuvers. But Tom,"

Ben's face suddenly drained of all its color, "what if it decides to launch us into null-space before we've tested the stardrive?"

Tom had been carefully studying a series of diagrams and equations on the viewscreen in front of him. "Stop me if I'm wrong, but if I read these fighter-class blueprints correctly, it would appear the battle subsystem contains two memories. One handles the fixed routines—like the ones being used now. The other one seems to be programable by updates from the bridge."

"You're right," Ben exclaimed after checking the information. "I'll input the equation to override the subsystem and—"

Both boys felt their stomachs lurch abruptly as the ship executed a roll with frightening speed, then nosed down into a sharp dive. Tom's eyes sought the monitor. He was shocked at the distance the *Exedra* had put between them and the threatening ship.

"Wow!" Tom exclaimed. "That should take care of our mystery pursuer for the moment. Now to deactivate that automatic battle subsystem. I trust my own abilities to handle the *Exedra* in a crisis more than the computer's judgment right now."

"I'll fix the computer," Ben muttered.

"If we ever needed your abilities, we need

them now, buddy," Tom urged. "We don't want to go for another ride like that."

"Or take a chance on the computer activating the stardrive until we test it," Ben added. "Did you get the registration number of the ship that caused all the trouble?"

"I wish I had," the blond boy said. "I'd like to file a formal complaint. We've been following our approved flight plan and this is certainly not restricted space. That pilot had no reason to threaten us."

"I think you'll get your wish to jot down his registration number," Ben said, pointing to the monitor. "He's back!"

"What does he think he's doing?" Tom exclaimed. "Have you found the manual override yet? I have a feeling the computer is going to take evasive action again just as soon as he gets a little closer."

"That's a fusion-drive ship, Tom, and it's going at its maximum speed just to catch up with us," Ben observed. "It seems like a terrific waste of fuel. They must think we're pretty important. At least we know one thing for sure."

"What's that?" his friend asked.

"That first attack was no accident. They're definitely after us or they would not be tailing us so frantically."

Tom frowned. "That's one piece of information I would be just as happy—"

Suddenly two flashes of light streaked from the sleek, gun-metal-gray mystery ship, heading for the *Exedra.*

"Those look like fusion torpedoes!" Ben exclaimed.

"They are," Tom replied. "We're being shot at!"

Chapter Two

"What's wrong with the battle computer, Ben? Why isn't it taking evasive action against those torpedoes?" Tom asked.

"I don't know, but—I've got it!" shouted the young computer tech triumphantly. "The *Exedra* is on manual now! She's all yours, Tom."

"Get set," the slender blond boy said tensely. "Here we go."

Tom nudged the *Exedra*'s acceleration control. The ship's drive responded instantly and the g-forces made him feel as if a great, invisible hand was suddenly pushing him back into his pilot's couch.

"If those are standard fusion torpedoes, then

they are heat-seeking, but their range is rather limited," he said to Ben. "We can outrun them easily, but we're very close to the edge of traffic around *New America*. The torpedoes won't be able to tell the heat given off by one ship from that of another. They only know to head in the direction of heat. If they get into the normal shipping lanes of *New America*, they're going to cause a lot of trouble! We'll have to lead them into deep space until their range is exhausted."

"Well, we wanted to test the ship's normal spacedrive," drawled Ben. "I suspect this is as good a time as any."

Tom leaned over the control panel and keyed the built-in radio microphone.

"This is Swift Enterprises' starship *Exedra*. Cease firing immediately and identify yourselves!"

There was no response from the mysterious attacker.

"They're blocking the ship-to-ship video signal, too," said Ben. "I guess they don't want to talk to us! Should I get the laser cannons ready?"

"No," Tom responded instantly. "That would be too dangerous. Just keep those torpedoes in sight and let's hope they fizzle out before we get too far out into space."

"Roger. I've got the rear cameras on them, Tom. They're—"

Suddenly the torpedoes exploded into two blinding flashes of light. A shadow fell across the bridge as the specially compounded glass of the ports compensated for the abrupt increase in the light level.

"They've self-destructed!" exclaimed Ben.

"This is getting more maddening by the second," said Tom, frowning. "Someone is playing—"

"*Exedra . . . Exedra.* Come in, *Exedra,*" the radio speaker suddenly boomed. "This is *New America* Traffic Control Station. Do you read me? *Exedra,* come in, please. Over."

Tom reached for the radio control. "*New America* Traffic Control, this is *Exedra.* We were just getting ready to call you. What's going on around here? Has war been declared against Swift Enterprises? Over."

"*Exedra,* what happened to you? We were tracking your approach and suddenly you zoomed off our screens so fast we couldn't follow you! We also registered an explosion of unknown origin near your coordinates. Please advise. Over."

"*New America,* we were being pursued and fired

upon by a fighter-class ship of unknown registration! Is it making a docking approach to the colony? Over."

There was a moment of silence and then a different, older-sounding voice spoke. "*Exedra*, stop playing games with us. You know very well that's impossible. What's really happening out there? Over."

Ben growled and started to pick up his co-pilot's microphone, but Tom motioned him to remain silent.

"*New America*, I am not joking. This is Tom Swift, pilot of the *Exedra*, and I hereby state into the formal record that we have been fired on by a ship of unknown origin. I repeat, is that fighter-class ship making a docking approach to the colony? Over."

"Negative, *Exedra*. No ship of that class is currently requesting approach data. Over." The voice of the traffic controller was emotionless.

"What?" shouted Ben. "Where did it go, then? It was here just a minute ago and now we've lost it from our screen! Over."

"Beg your pardon, *Exedra*?" asked Traffic Control. "Do you have the registration number of the vessel in question? Over."

"Look here, you," Ben began spluttering, "we just told you—"

Tom put a hand on his friend's shoulder. "We must have made an error, Control," the young inventor said into his mike. "Request permission to dock. Over."

"Stand by for flash transmission of essential data. Over."

Tom flicked a switch. "Proceed, *New America.* Over."

A light blinked, signifying that a complicated mathematical message had been sent from *New America* Control to the ship's computer. A second later, a green light went on, indicating the end of the transmission. Tom thanked the controller and pressed a button to close the channel.

"There was no use arguing with them, Ben. It must have been some sort of military foul-up and you know those things are classified until they're sorted out. We'll probably receive an official apology in a few days. Perhaps I can ask my father to check with his military contacts to see what happened."

The young inventor breathed a sigh of exhaustion and unbuckled his restraining harness. "How about taking over for awhile now? I'm beat."

Ben grinned. "You figure I need the experience, huh? Okay, sure." He busied himself with the controls for a moment, then added, "I think

I'll play with the battle computer and work on programing it to suit the new *Exedra*. We don't need any more surprises like the last one."

"Good idea," Tom responded and pushed himself out of the couch. He twisted effortlessly in the weightless condition and grabbed a hand-hold which was molded into the ship's bulkhead. "I'm going to stretch my legs a bit. You might put in a call to Anita and Aristotle so they'll be ready to leave when we get there. I'm anxious to continue our experiment!"

The young inventor's voice grew serious. "Dad wanted us to make this ship operational as soon as possible. I think he's beginning to worry about security. There are a lot of people who wouldn't mind knowing the secret of the alien stardrive. I wonder if the mysterious attack just now was connected somehow with the drive?"

"Perhaps," Ben answered. "We both know some people aren't too particular about how they get something they want desperately! I haven't forgotten the great lengths David Luna went to to secure the stardrive for his company."

Luna was a powerful, wealthy businessman who had stolen the alien probe from Swift Enterprises shortly after the young people had brought it back from Io. After much adventure and excitement, (as told in *Tom Swift: The Alien*

Probe), the young people barely escaped the clutches of the ruthless man.

"Well, we don't have to worry about Mister Luna anymore," Ben observed.

"I wish I knew that for sure!" said Tom, frowning worriedly. "He just disappeared. We don't know if he's dead or alive."

"Without the Luna Corporation, David Luna has no power. Even if he is alive, there's nothing he can do now," Ben insisted.

"Since he's been missing, the corporation's dealings have been watched very closely," Tom declared. "The new chairman of the board doesn't appear to have any secrets or any interest in expanding the corporation's holdings. Outwardly, at least, all their energy is going into maintaining their present activities."

"But you still don't trust them, do you?" Ben asked.

"No. David Luna is one of the most brilliant and dangerous men I've ever met. If there's any way he can secretly manipulate the resources of the Luna Corporation, I'm sure he will." Tom floated toward the doorway. "I'm going aft for a while. Call me when we get to *New America*."

"Sure, buddy. Take it easy," Ben replied.

Tom pushed off from a nearby bulkhead and propelled himself into the ship's main cabin. The plush luxuriousness of it almost made him forget his anxieties about the mysterious ship and David Luna. The *Exedra* was a far cry from the usual scientific research ship.

During the modification and general overhaul, when the stardrive was installed, Tom had added interior conveniences to better suit his needs and those of his friends. The most extensive of these had been the expansion of the ship's library, including the latest complete *Encyclopedia Galactica* on microfiche.

Fortunately for the appetites of everyone on board, the ship's previous owner had been something of a gourmet cook. He had insisted that the galley be as completely equipped as his kitchen on Earth. Tom only had to make sure that it was fully stocked for weightless cooking as well as planetside eating.

The young inventor hesitated, floating in the corridor between the cabin he shared with Ben and the lab.

Unfortunately, privacy had been one of the sacrifices required of everyone to accommodate the stardrive. All rear cabins had been eliminated and that meant doubling-up in the forward cabins. But he had not had the heart to take out the giant bathtub that Anita loved so much. And since Aristotle did not sleep, Anita had a cabin to herself.

Tom opened the door to his cabin and looked at his bed which seemed very inviting. But the restless, inventive energy that was so much a part of him won out. He went into the lab.

Everything there was designed for the weightlessness of space as well as the gravity of planetside docking. Using the handholds, Tom guided himself to his work area and strapped himself in. In his mind, this was "down" and he could then easily orient himself to the rest of the lab.

Deciding what was "up" and what was "down" was one of the problems with weightless living. Unless people oriented themselves, living without gravity could cause dizziness and headaches.

Another problem was that things floated away unless they were secured to a surface in some way.

Tom released a clamp on his workbench and quickly reached out to catch the small, featureless black plastic square that drifted in front of him. It was his latest invention, the "translator-teacher." Two others, in various stages of completion, were still clamped to the bench.

He had developed the translator-teacher to do exactly what its name implied. He, Ben, and

Anita would have to use it once they got to the Skree system because Aristotle could not be everywhere at once and, right now, the robot was their only means of communicating with the Skree.

Tom turned the black square over in his hand. He was rather proud of the thought and care that had gone into it. The device could be worn on any part of the body, even under clothing or connected to spacesuit radios. It was a tiny microcomputer that could either be tied to Aristotle's memory or function independently. It would translate another language instantly and, by means of a small loudspeaker, would also make it possible for aliens to understand what the humans were saying. When two or more units were close together, they could exchange information by microwave transmission. They could also go to Aristotle for vocabulary updates and to enlarge his own memory.

In short, the units would have the same language proficiency as Aristotle, and the robot's vocabulary would be expanded as well.

Translation was the main function of the device, but Tom hated the thought of being totally dependent on any artificial brain—even Aristotle's. So the translator-teacher, T-T for short, would also teach the foreign language to the wearer while he or she was sleeping.

Tom exposed the circuitry of the device in his hand and pulled out his micro-soldering tools. Fortunately, nuts-and-bolts work like this didn't take all of his concentration and he let his mind wander to the situation he and his friends were about to face.

The Skree and the Chutans were unknown races. He didn't even know what they looked like. It was obvious, however, that the Skree were intelligent and scientifically advanced. The probe they had sent into the Sol system had certainly been highly sophisticated. If the Chutans could keep up a war against such people for a long time, then they, too, were presumably intelligent.

The fact that the two races were at war with each other bothered Tom. Who knew what kinds of weapons were being used? How would he and his friends protect themselves against weapons they had never even seen? Frankly, it scared him.

"Hey, Tom," Ben said over the intercom. "We're coming in."

Tom felt the gravity slowly returning as the ship braked for its rendezvous with *New America* and the lab began to have a floor and ceiling that was not merely illusionary once again.

The young inventor hurried into the cockpit, strapped himself in, and looked out of the port at the approaching dot that was the cylindrical world of *New America*. It spun slowly in the sky before them.

"We're on automatic now," Ben said. "I'm going aft to clean up. How about you?"

Tom winked at his friend. "I think I'll sit here and watch. Sometimes you computer jockeys miss a decimal point in your fancy calculations. Then we pilots have to be ready to clean up your mess!"

Besides, Tom thought to himself, this is the last stop before the trip which will at last connect man with intelligent life—somewhere out there in the stars!

Chapter Three

Aristotle was waiting for the boys at the landing dock. As they walked up to the squat mechanoid, they grinned broadly. Tom had to restrain himself from giving his robot a big hug. After all, he thought, he would not hug his spaceship or his motorcycle.

But then, Aristotle had always seemed to Tom to be human. Ever since the young inventor had built him, the mechanoid had been something more than a highly sophisticated collection of metal parts and rubber hoses.

"Aristotle!" Ben exclaimed exuberantly. "It's good to see you, you old bucket of bolts. Who

27

would have thought we would miss you so much?" The computer tech threw his arms around the robot in a fierce, playful bear hug.

Tom's grin widened even more as Aristotle submitted to Ben's greeting. "I have missed you too, Ben," the mechanoid replied. "Anita and I have suffered by foregoing the pleasure of your company. Nevertheless, we have both remained very active while awaiting this reunion."

Tom looked around the dock area. "Speaking of Anita, where is she?" he asked.

"She requested that I let you know she will be here very shortly. There are three final tests on the new parts she wished to run. Though either the computer aboard *Exedra* or the computer in her leg would be adequate to correlate the data, she thought it would only be prudent to use the facilities of the much larger computer here since it is available."

Several years before, Anita Thorwald had suffered a crippling accident. Doctors had been forced to remove her right leg below the knee but had replaced it with an artificial limb that housed a sophisticated computer. It was connected with the redhead's nervous system which enabled her to sense the floor beneath her artificial foot and gave her an even greater ability in athletics than before.

It also made the girl extremely sensitive to other people's emotions. As an empath, her heightened awareness allowed her to read other people's feelings but not their minds.

Tom thought for a moment, then said, "I'm going to call my father and let him know about the attack on the *Exedra* and the disappearance of the fighter ship."

Aristotle's lights blinked in concern. "What attack? What ship? Have you suffered damage?"

"Ben will fill you in. I'll be right back," Tom responded, then jogged to the Interplanetary Communications Center.

A few minutes later, after giving his father the news and assuring him they would take every precaution they could, Tom returned to the docking area to discover Ben and Aristotle gone and a stranger nosing about the *Exedra* in a suspicious manner.

"What's going on here?" the young inventor asked sternly.

"Are you Tom Swift?" the stranger asked with a smirk.

"That's right," Tom replied. "What are you doing here?"

"You gotta show me your pest-inspection certificate," the man replied, ignoring Tom's question. "You don't do that, you're not goin' nowhere in this here ship."

The clean, recycled air of the *New America* Space Dock suddenly seemed oppressive and stifling to Tom. He stared at the stocky, swaggering dock attendant in anger and disbelief.

"We need a pest-inspection certificate? I don't think you understand. We're going into deep space to test some scientific equipment." He pulled a bundle of legal forms and certificates from one of the pockets of his jumpsuit and showed them to the man. "Here are all the documents we need." Tom said.

"I've got my orders from Port Authority, Mister," insisted the man whose name tag read GARCIA. "These orders say this here *Exedra* is gotta be declared free of insect pests and vermin before leavin' port. Seems you got a substantial cargo of food products aboard."

"The food aboard the *Exedra* is not cargo!" Tom protested. "Those are our supplies. We're not selling them to anyone and whoever listed them as cargo made a mistake."

"Don't know about that. I don't give the orders, I just follow 'em," Garcia said in a bored voice. "You've gotta get an inspector from Pest Control to give you a pest-inspection certificate or else you're not leavin' here."

Tom noticed that a few people in the lounge were staring at them and he lowered his voice. He wanted to maintain a low profile and not call any more attention to either himself or their ship than was absolutely necessary.

"We already have permission to conduct a scientific test beginning in this area," he explained tensely.

"Sorry," said Garcia. "You still need a Pest Control certificate."

Tom could tell that the man wasn't sorry at all and he turned away to control his rising temper. Then he saw Anita Thorwald striding toward him. The beautiful and quick-tempered redhead was obviously picking up the strong emotions generated by his argument with Garcia because she, too, looked angry!

The young inventor searched his mind for a way of bypassing what was obviously a skillfully and deliberately placed bureaucratic roadblock. "Is there anyone I can talk to about this?" he asked.

Garcia's expression instantly hardened. "You want to go over my head, eh? Well, it ain't gonna do you no good 'cause—"

"What's the problem?" Anita interrupted. Her large green eyes flashed from Tom to Garcia and back again. Garcia looked at her with a puzzled expression on his face. Tom realized that the man was probably wondering why Anita, whom he had never seen before, was boiling mad at him.

"Someone has made sure that we're not leaving *New America* until he decides it's okay," Tom replied. "We've had a technicality pulled on us. Our supplies have been listed as cargo."

Anita whistled softly. "That's going to be a hard one to beat," she said.

Garcia was beginning to look uncomfortable. Tom decided to try a different approach. "I'd like to know who issued that order and why," he told Garcia as calmly as he could.

Instead of answering, the man stared past him with an uncertain frown replacing his look of swaggering confidence. Tom turned to see Ben and Aristotle approaching them.

"As I was saying . . ." began Tom, but he stopped in mid-sentence. He knew he had lost the man's attention.

"Under *New American* law, we have the right to know who issued the order for a pest inspection," Anita spoke up.

Garcia backed away nervously.

"Wait," said Tom.

"Talk to my supervisors!" the dark attendant blurted as he turned and cut through a crowd of

people gathered around an information holo-
gram. Tom started to follow the man, but gave
up. Garcia was obviously experienced at losing
himself in a crowd.

"Did we interrupt something?" Ben asked.

Tom explained the situation and Ben shook
his head, bewildered. "I'm sorry we intimidated
him before you found out what you wanted to
know," he said.

"I do not think intimidation was the reason for
the man's rapid departure," said Aristotle. "It is
highly probable that he has the information you
requested, but he was not prepared by his superior for a confrontation with a group."

"There's something going on here that I don't
like," Tom said, frowning.

"Let's pay a visit to the Pest Control offices
and straighten this mess out so we can get on
with our test," Ben suggested.

"I don't think we should all go," Tom commented. "I suddenly don't like the idea of leaving the ship unguarded. I'd feel more at ease if
you, Anita, and Aristotle stayed here with the *Exedra*. Don't let *anyone* aboard if you can help it."

"You don't know *New America* well enough to
find Pest Control by yourself," Anita spoke up.
"I'm going with you."

Tom knew better than to argue with Anita—

especially when she was right, as she was now.

The two young people took an electric tram from the boarding lounge and got off at Industry Avenue, one of the main streets of the colony.

"This area is off limits to mechanized traffic," Anita told Tom. "We'll have to walk the rest of the way."

Tom had never been to this section of the colony. It was devoted mainly to light industry and, normally, he would have no reason to go there. He looked around, familiarizing himself with the new terrain. It felt good to be back in the city in space.

Tom Swift had lived with the excitement of *New America* since childhood. It had been conceived by his father and built by a Swift Enterprises team of scientists, engineers, and technicians. Tom could not remember a time when the problems and triumphs of the project had not been dinner-table conversation in the Swift household. A man-made world in which 200,000 people lived and worked!

Inside, *New America* always reminded Tom of the huge, old-style shopping malls on Earth. The floor was carefully landscaped and the colony offered a variety of goods and services to its inhabitants in a weatherproof, compressed space.

New America was a cylinder a mile in diameter

and three miles long which rotated on its axis once every 114 seconds. This created a gravity much like Earth's on the perimeter of the cylinder where the colonists lived.

Banks of mirrored panels ringed the outside of the cylinder and directed sunlight into the interior through long, slotlike windows. They were controlled by a computer to simulate night and day as well as the four seasons. This was mainly for the benefit of the plant life and the psychological well-being of the Earth-born colonists. Yet, there was already a generation born on *New America* that did not know what it was like to live according to the whims of natural weather.

"Look," said Anita, pointing at a dome-shaped structure, "that's Thorwald Engineering!"

Anita had lived most of her life on *New America* and preferred it to Earth. Her family had been one of the first to emigrate to the space colony, attracted by the low-gravity conditions which were ideal for the manufacture of products such as perfect ball bearings, medicines, and incredibly strong, lightweight building materials.

After she, Tom, and Ben had become friends, they had built *Aristotle*. They had shared many adventures and each new experience had linked them even closer together. Their friendship was a solid chain forged by danger, excitement, and discovery. Tom's heart warmed as his mind traveled back into the past.

Anita looked at him and smiled. "We've had good times together, haven't we?" she asked.

Tom blushed. "I keep forgetting that you can read emotions," he stammered, a little embarrassed.

Anita laughed. "You should know by now that you can't hide anything from me!" Then she pointed at a squat, horseshoe-shaped building ten yards ahead of them. "The Pest Control offices are in there," she said.

The structure's architecture was clean and simple. In the center of the horseshoe was a beautifully landscaped park. Tom felt a gentle breeze ruffle his hair and he took a deep breath, savoring the scent of the flowers nearby.

Suddenly he felt the firm pressure of a hand on his shoulder. He stiffened. Anita gasped with alarm at the same time. Her empathic powers had sensed trouble behind them.

"Pretend nothing is wrong," whispered Ben Walking Eagle, "but we've got to leave *New America* at once!"

Chapter Four

"Keep walking, everyone," Ben urged. "We're probably under surveillance right now."

"Is the *Exedra* all right?" Tom asked, forcing a smile, even though that was the last thing he felt like doing.

"Aristotle is there," Ben replied. "He said he would play 'dumb robot' if anyone tries to board the ship."

"What's going on?" asked Anita. "Can we turn around now?"

Ben nodded and then grinned at a tall, slim woman standing a short distance behind them. "I'd like you to meet my cousin, Katherine Reiko One Star," he said to his friends.

Tom stared at her in surprise. The woman was heavily armed with some of the latest and most powerful hand weapons on the market, including a Smith & Wesson needle gun!

"Kate was waiting for me when Aristotle and I arrived on board the ship," Ben explained. "She came to warn me that if we don't get ourselves and the *Exedra* out of *New America* immediately, we'll never get the ship into space again!"

Anita could not hold back a small cry of dismay.

"I'll explain everything later," Kate spoke with crisp authority. "Right now we'd better head for your ship. We'll have to proceed slowly so that no one will suspect there is anything wrong. Just act as though we're all old friends out for a leisurely stroll."

The four young people headed back in the direction of the tram. They walked casually and passers-by seemed not to notice anything unusual about them, though quite a few gaped at Kate One Star.

Although Tom laughed and appeared to be enjoying himself, the bright, clean avenues of *New America* had suddenly become a sinister labyrinth. He wondered if the delicate architecture and beautiful landscaping of this space colony might hide attackers or thugs.

"How does your cousin know so much about the danger we're in?" Anita asked Ben.

Tom could sense that the volatile redhead was not willing to trust Kate One Star completely. Was it jealousy? He had never known Anita to give in to emotions in a real crisis. But he had to admit that the strange young woman Ben had called his cousin was exotically beautiful.

Her muscular but well-proportioned and voluptuous figure was apparent in the snug-fitting black jumper that she wore. It was obviously some kind of uniform, since it had epaulets with an insignia that Tom did not recognize—a white circle with a sword through it against a speckled background.

Her waist-length, blue-black hair was straight. Kate wore it loose and parted in the middle so that it accented her high cheekbones and dark, almond-shaped eyes. Her skin was a darker shade than Ben's and Tom noticed a slight oriental cast to her features. With a middle name like Reiko she might be partially Japanese, Tom thought.

If the young woman was aware of any hostility from Anita, she did not show it. "I know about the danger you are in because I was hired to prevent you and your ship from leaving *New America*," she explained matter-of-factly.

"What?" Anita exploded. "We're putting ourselves into the hands of the enemy?"

"Keep your voice down!" Ben hissed.

"I'm a free-lance combat specialist," Kate explained. "When I was offered this job, I was told that your departure from New America would endanger the colony and all its inhabitants. However, when I saw Ben's name on the ship's manifest, I realized that I had been lied to and that I could not fulfill my contract. I decided to warn you of the situation."

"Did the manifest say anything about a missing Pest Control certificate?" Tom inquired.

Kate shrugged. "I don't remember. The Pest Control certificate was brought up only as a tactic designed to delay and confuse you momentarily until we'd get into position. Even if you had corrected the error, you would not have been allowed to leave," she explained.

"Who's your employer?" Tom asked.

"I-I can't tell you," Kate stammered. It was the first time that Tom had heard any uncertainty in the young woman's voice. Obviously her employer was an extremely powerful person.

"I was sworn to secrecy," she explained. "I took an oath and I must abide by it."

"Then how can you expect us to trust you?" Anita asked.

"I wouldn't want you to do anything that might compromise your personal integrity," Tom said thoughtfully. "But it would certainly help us to know who is behind all of this. If I take a guess and I am right, will you tell me?"

"I suppose that would not be a breach of my oath," Kate replied slowly.

"This is silly," Anita muttered.

"Am I correct in assuming that you're wearing a uniform and that it was given to you as a part of this assignment?" Tom began.

"Yes."

"Then the insignia on the epaulets is that of your employer?"

"Yes," Kate said again.

"The background looks like stars," said Anita. "Could that white circle represent a planet?"

"Or a moon?" Tom asked. "Are you employed by the Luna Corporation?"

"No."

"Who else would know about the *Exedra* and want to stop us?" asked Ben.

"I think those two guys coming toward us might," said Anita. "Either they're working for the same outfit, or it's uniform day on *New America*."

Tom watched the two men approach. They obviously were wary and ready for trouble.

"Let me handle this," said Kate. "Apparently there has been a change in strategy. Kregar and Stephens shouldn't be here. We were told to maintain a low profile until we secured the ship."

"Tell me something," said Tom. "How is it that someone can send a private army—that's what you and your friends are—up to *New America* to conduct a campaign against a group of free citizens and their ship and not get into trouble?"

"If your analysis of the situation is correct, Mister Swift—and it is correct—then there can be only one answer," said Kate.

Anita hissed angrily, "You mean—there are some official backs turned."

"Obviously," said Kate One Star. Without further comment, she motioned for Tom, Ben, and Anita to stop. She took a few steps forward to suggest to her two colleagues that she was in control, then waited for them to approach. They saluted her and she returned the salute.

"It's all very military, isn't it?" whispered Anita.

"Shhhhhh!" said Tom. "I'm trying to hear what they're saying."

Kate and the two men were speaking in low tones and he only caught an occasional word. However, from their body language, the young inventor could tell that they did not like what Kate was telling them. They kept glancing suspiciously at the young people.

Finally, Kate turned quickly on her heel and walked back to the group, followed by Kregar and Stephens.

"I don't think there is anything you can do to help," Tom heard the young woman say. He noticed she was looking intently at Ben. "Mister Walking Eagle is ill," she went on. "In fact, he's so ill he just might collapse at any moment!"

Suddenly Ben clutched his side and began moaning as though suffering an attack of appendicitis. Out of the corner of his eye, Tom saw Anita pick up the cue immediately. The alert redhead rushed to Ben's side to comfort him.

Tom decided to get into the drama, too. He gave the two men what he hoped was his most reproving frown. "Now look what you've done! Get out of the way! We have to take this man to a doctor at once!"

The ruse was working. The tough men looked thoroughly confused and uncertain about what action to take. One of them, a tall, husky man with thinning brown hair, stepped up to Ben and peered into the young man's face.

"He doesn't look sick to me," he declared.

"Since when is the appendix located in the face?" Kate demanded. "Do you have a medical degree, Kregar?"

"No," the man snarled. "Me and Stephens just want to make sure that we earn a lot of pay points on this assignment."

"Yeah," agreed Stephens, a dark-haired, wiry man. He had a nervous tick that made him wink frequently. Tom found it disconcerting. "We wouldn't want to think that one person was going to get all the bonus money."

Ben groaned so dramatically that Tom turned in alarm. Kate motioned for him and Anita to help their sick friend walk.

Kregar and Stephens stepped in front of them to block their way. Kate appeared not to notice. Instead, she put a hand on Ben's shoulder.

With a sudden whoop, Ben charged directly into the two men, catching them off guard. Stephens jumped back, cursing and reaching for the butt of his needle gun. Before he could get it out, Kate landed a powerful sidekick directly on his elbow. Tom heard the joint break and Stephens howled in pain. He sank to his knees clutching his lifeless arm. Kate lunged in and sent him to the ground with an open-palm karate chop to the neck.

Kregar had drawn his laser. Without waiting to

consider the danger involved, Tom stepped up to the man and swung a lower block across Kregar's gun arm. A burst of laser fire hit some decorative rock and burned it.

While the man was bent over, Tom grasped him by the back of the neck and shoved his knee into Kregar's chin. The man went limp and collapsed to the ground.

"Grab their guns!" shouted Kate. "The game is up now. We've got to get back to your ship as fast as possible."

Tom and Ben removed the guns from their two adversaries. Unfortunately, the fight had drawn a small crowd and the young people knew that their escape would have many witnesses.

"The tram will be too slow. We'd better take the service passages to the dock. Follow me!" Anita shouted and ran toward a pair of doors to her left.

Tom moved up beside Kate as the group made their way quickly to the end of the cylindrical space colony. "That trick you and Ben pulled off went like clockwork. You've done it before, haven't you?" Tom inquired.

"Yes, but not since we were kids. I was hoping Ben would remember the signals," Kate said.

"In all the time I've known him, Ben never mentioned that he had a cousin in the—"

"Free-lance combat specialist business?" Kate finished, smiling. "That's because the family doesn't talk about me. I'm something of an embarrassment to them."

"I'm sure Ben doesn't feel that way," Tom said.

"You're right. Ben and I have always been close. He never criticized me when I joined the marines and he stuck by me after I got out and took up the combat trade," explained Kate.

"Why did you go into it?" Tom asked.

"I've always been a fighter. I get it from both sides of the family. My mother can trace her ancestors back through several samurai warlords and my father, Ben's uncle, is the oldest of the clan. That makes him a war chief.

"It's not that I actually love to fight," the girl continued. "It just comes with the job. What I like is the excitement and the adventure of going into a dangerous situation."

Tom laughed. "Well, you've certainly gotten yourself into one this time."

In the distance behind them, they heard the high-pitched squeal of an alert siren.

"Kregar and Stephens must have turned in an alarm," Anita exclaimed.

"I don't think so," said Kate. "That would draw too much attention to them and to the presence of an organized military group on *New America*. Someone may have done it for them, however. Is your ship ready to blast out of here?"

"If I know Aristotle, he's been monitoring all the communications around here," Tom replied. "He's probably better informed than anybody, so if the situation is getting hot for us, he'll have the ship ready."

"Things are growing uncomfortably warm already" Ben spoke up.

"We're almost to the docking area," Anita told the others. "Just up that ramp and through the doors."

The young people increased their speed and soon reached the dock where the *Exedra* was waiting.

Aristotle appeared in the entranceway. "Hurry," he urged them. "Danger is immediately behind you."

Tom risked a quick look back and what he saw chilled him!

Chapter Five

An electric tram with armed security guards was rapidly approaching behind him!

"Run!" Tom yelled.

The four raced through the entrance to *Exedra* and began to prepare for an immediate takeoff.

Tom thumbed a switch sealing the ship's outer hatch and watched impatiently as the robot boarding tube retracted into the colony's flight tower. "Is everyone strapped in?" he asked, not taking his eyes from the control panel.

On the monitor, Ben saw the guards jump from the slowing tram and thunder to the docking slip. When they discovered that the boarding tube was no longer attached to the *Exedra,* one of them spoke into a communicator. Ben guessed the man was alerting his superiors to the situation. The young computer tech knew police cruisers would be after the *Exedra* within seconds.

Tom's hand hesitated over the release for the ship's electromagnetic grapples. "Shall we clear our departure with the control tower? I feel peculiar making an unauthorized liftoff like this!"

"If you ask them, they're going to say no. Then what'll you do?" Anita asked.

"You're right," the young inventor replied. "But we'll get into much trouble for this!"

"We're already in a heap of trouble. Let's get out of here while we still can!" Ben advised. "In about 90 seconds it might be too late," he added, thinking about the police ships which should be appearing at any moment.

Tom pulled the release, shutting off the current to the *Exedra*'s half of the launch deck anchor and they floated free of the rotating colony. Then he gently coaxed the solid-fuel attitude engines and readied the ship for drive engagement.

"Incidentally, Tom," Aristotle said, "have you given any thought as to where we are going?" The squat mechanoid had locked his motorframe to the bulkhead and his hands were on the controls of the spaceship's navigational equipment.

Only his sensorframe, housing his two camera eyes and his other sensors, was turned toward his creator.

Tom firmly pulled on the acceleration control and the ship responded and flew upward. G-forces pushed the passengers deep into their padded couches. He coaxed every bit of speed from the powerful engines and put as much distance as possible between the *Exedra* and *New America.*

"We're going back to Earth!" Tom announced. "I'll contact my father and tell him what's going on."

"This may be too big for even your father to deal with, Tom," Ben suggested.

"Now that we've left *New America,* our troubles have only begun," said Kate One Star. "In space, there are no laws to protect us."

Aristotle broke into the discussion. "My instruments show that we are already being pursued. There are five ships—one large and four that are smaller. They are police cruisers."

"The larger vessel is probably the *Roxanne,*" Kate put in. "My employer will stop at nothing to get this ship and the crew of the *Roxanne* thinks you are unarmed. They know a great deal about your capabilities although they don't understand the nature of the stardrive. Based on what I know of the ship's commander, they'll try to disable the *Exedra* if they have to in order to capture it."

"Was the *Roxanne* the ship that fired on us when we were approaching *New America?*" Tom asked.

Kate nodded.

"You were aboard it, weren't you?" he asked.

"Yes, although I had nothing to do with the launching of the torpedoes. I thought it was reckless and voted against it. After that, I realized I had gotten myself into a group that was more foolhardy than professional," Kate explained.

"There certainly were some official backs turned," Tom commented. "But then we all know that the current director of *New America* once worked for David Luna. This sort of intrigue happened to us once before when we were trying to get the alien probe back after Luna had stolen it. I'm beginning to suspect the effusive Mr. Luna has not given up his quest to get the secret of the stardrive."

"He hasn't," said Kate. "You've guessed my employer and I told you if you guessed correctly, I would tell you."

"Before you insisted that you didn't work for Luna!" Anita said sharply.

"I said I didn't work for the Luna Corporation," Kate corrected her. "And I don't. Right now David Luna has nothing to do with the company. He hired me personally."

"How could you work for someone as evil as that man?" Anita asked. "Don't you have any sense of personal honor?"

"Anita!" Tom exclaimed.

"Her attitude is understandable," Kate said. "But I didn't realize what Luna was up to until today."

Anita frowned and leaned over to stare at the insignia on Kate's uniform. "Luna has never used this emblem before. The sword piercing the white circle—which is obviously a moon—is a corny touch, but the meaning is absolutely clear to me. He means to control as large a chunk of the galaxy as possible. That man doesn't dream on a small scale and the stardrive is the key to his plans of conquest," Anita said.

"If all this is true, then I'm going to put some distance between us and our pursuers before we decide what to do," Tom said. "Grab oxygen masks because the g-forces might make breathing difficult. We'll make a fast run into deep space."

When he was sure everyone was prepared, Tom pulled on the ship's acceleration control.

The stars gradually became more and more elongated. Suddenly they turned into brilliant streaks of light, flashing past the ports like bright pins.

Tom felt a tightness in his chest and was thankful for the oxygen mask. Although they were well under the speed of light and were not yet testing the stardrive, the *Exedra* was traveling faster than any ship ever made by human beings.

The young inventor heard the thermostatic controls kick in. Louvers all over the ship would be opening, dissipating the high hull temperatures into space, while coolers labored to keep the interior temperature within human tolerance.

Tom heard a roaring sound from the pressure outside as he adjusted the controls to a slightly lower cruising speed. They were still going much faster than the *Roxanne*. The orange hue of Mars shone dimly from the front camera monitors.

After an hour, he slowed the ship even more. They all removed their oxygen masks. Kate One Star wiped the perspiration from her forehead and took several deep breaths. "I was told what this ship might be capable of, but I didn't believe it!" she said.

"There is no sign of pursuit, Tom," Aristotle spoke up. "We gave them the slip."

"Of course we did." Ben laughed. "It'll be a good while before they show up on our instruments again and then only if we slow down. But what are we going to do now? There's no place to go. We can stay in space until our food gives out, but we'll have to go back to Earth or *New America* sometime."

"We do have another alternative," Tom said quietly. "We can always carry out the mission for which we rebuilt this ship."

"You mean, make the jump to Alpha Centauri and go in search of the Skree?" asked Ben.

"Jump? Skree? Alpha Centauri? What are you talking about?" Kate asked excitedly.

"We found a probe sent from the Alpha Centauri system by a race of beings called the Skree," Tom explained. "In a nutshell, they need help in fighting another group of aliens, the Chutans, who are after their planet, Skranipor. We had planned to test the stardrive on the way to the Skree, and if we manage to make contact with them, perhaps we can figure out a way to help them."

Kate looked shocked. "But this ship can't get mixed up in a war!" she protested. "It's only armed with some laser cannons and none of you have had an ounce of military experience! It's insane."

"I was a boy scout, remember?" Ben teased her.

Kate gave her cousin a withering look. "This is serious."

Anita broke in. "Wait a minute. You are both forgetting something very important. We are volunteers for this trip, but Kate isn't. She's here by accident. We can't just drop her off at the nearest asteroid or expect her to go along with our experiment, given all the unknown dangers."

"You're right," said Tom. "We'll go back to Earth. Ben, set a course for the Shopton, New Mexico complex and get my father on the horn. Perhaps they'll have some ideas."

"Not so fast," Kate said quickly. "I've got nothing to go back for. There's no real adventure left on Earth. There's no more unexplored territory to open up for settlers, no more frontiers for me to explore or tame."

Tom, Ben, and Anita looked at her expectantly.

"I don't know about the Skree or the Chutans," the girl went on, "but I do know about war. That's where you're going, right into war. You need me and the experience I have and I need you because, frankly, things are going to be pretty hot for me on Earth. Luna will have a bunch of henchmen searching for me all over the globe and *New America.*"

Ben took his cousin's hand into his and there

was concern in his voice as he spoke. "I hadn't even thought of that, but you're right. It'll be very dangerous for you."

Kate nodded. "Therefore, I propose to take the job of military advisor to this expedition. I want to go with you."

"That's very generous of you," said Tom. "But this is not just a space jaunt with some aliens at the other end of the trip. Before you make up your mind, you have to know exactly what you're getting into. After all, one of the main points of military strategy is to be aware of the forces you are up against, right?"

" 'Know the enemy' is the first law of the military," Kate agreed.

"Well, the stardrive is not an enemy, but it is largely unknown and has great potential danger for us all," Tom explained. He turned to the robot. "Aristotle, keep an eye out for any sign of our pursuers. I doubt we will be bothered by them again, but it would be foolish to take any chances."

"My sensors indicate no activity in this quadrant of space, but I shall, nevertheless, keep a close watch," the mechanoid said.

"Okay." Tom unbuckled his restraining harness. "I think we should all go into the lounge right now and carefully consider our situation."

"Oh, Tom," Aristotle called as the young inventor began floating toward the back of the cabin. "I realize that technically I am not entitled to a vote as I am not a human being. However, I would like to volunteer to continue the mission to the Skree if that is the decision of the group."

Tom grinned at the robot, a lump of emotion suddenly making his throat feel tight. "Thanks, pal. I appreciate the vote of confidence."

As the young people settled into their seats in the luxurious lounge, Tom tried to describe the stardrive to Kate, whose scientific background was limited.

"For years scientists were convinced that nothing could go faster than light. They didn't believe in such a thing as null-space. The universe was as we saw it. There was nothing else."

"Wait a minute," Kate interrupted, "you're losing me already. I follow you about the universe being the way we saw it. But what's this null-space thing?"

Tom knitted his brow in concentration. "Well, according to Skree scientists, there is space and there is non-space. Non-space is outside the space we see and it vibrates at a totally different rate. That's why we can't see it."

"If we could vibrate at the same speed as null-space, then we would see null-space rather than the space we are familiar with," Ben put in.

"Wait, wait, wait!" Kate held up her hand. "Are you trying to tell me there's something all around us we can't see because it vibrates differently than we do?"

Tom nodded.

"That sounds like you're talking about another reality—a fourth dimension!" Kate exclaimed.

"That's one way of putting it," Tom agreed.

Kate looked at Ben and Anita. "Do you two go along with this?"

"Theoretically it's possible," said Ben. "The stardrive creates an electromagnetic field around the entire ship which acts as a crowbar. When the ship moves forward, it slips into null-space through the crack the 'crowbar' has wedged between real space and null-space."

Kate sat still for a moment. "So this electromagnetic field makes it possible for us to go from one dimension into the next. Sort of pop from one part of the universe over to another by a process we don't really understand."

"That's one of the big dangers," Tom said. "We've only been able to speculate about this theoretically. Everyone agrees on the theory. But maybe we won't come out on the other side. Perhaps we'll be trapped."

Kate stared at him. "Trapped?"

"Trapped in a moment of time—or non-time—forever!" Tom said.

Chapter Six

"You mean—" the young woman whispered, "we might end up frozen in limbo?"

"Exactly," her cousin answered.

Kate One Star leaned back in her chair. "Why not experiment first with animals, the way scientists did back in the twentieth century when they sent monkeys up in space capsules to make sure it was safe?"

"Those scientists could keep track of the capsules at all times," Tom explained. "They could monitor everything. Unfortunately, we are dealing with null-space. We're not sure where we will end up and certainly our equipment could not track anything jumping through the universe that way."

"The only thing to do is to try it," Anita added.

Ben looked at his cousin gravely. "So you see, Kate, this is not just a long space trip. It's much more than that and we really can't ask you to come along."

Kate was quiet for a few minutes, her head bowed in deep thought. Finally she looked at the others. "I've made up my mind," she said. "I want to go with you."

"Agreed," said Tom. "Any objections?" he asked Ben and Anita. There were none. "Then it's settled."

Anita turned to Kate. "You can bunk with me, since I have the only single cabin."

Tom was grateful for this overture of friendship on the redhead's part and Kate was aware of the peacemaking gesture as well.

"Thank you, Anita. That's very kind of you." The two girls smiled at each other.

Tom turned to Ben. "You'd better go into the cockpit with Aristotle and start calculating the jump. Use the information that the probe supplied. I'll help you as soon as I beam a message to my father, letting him know we're going ahead immediately on our stardrive mission."

Kate stood up. "My first suggestion as military advisor is that Anita and I comb the ship for all the weapons on board. I want to see exactly what we have so I can decide on the best deployment of the troops if it comes to an actual shooting fight."

"What she means is that she wants to know just how hopeless this crew is as an army," Anita said wryly.

Tom laughed. "We'll all meet back here in two hours."

"This is it, huh?" asked Kate, shaking her head. "Three hand lasers, three needle guns besides my own, seven ammo clips, a buck knife, two packages of matches, three paring knives, and a set of silverware. I can't believe you were actually planning on charging into a war in space with this stuff!"

"We're not prepared for an all-out military campaign," Tom said. "But remember, our main purpose is to test the drive system. In the process we are trying to locate the Skree and find out what is going on. We're not planning to join in their war against the Chutans at this time. How could we? We can't face alien weapons when we know so little about the beings who made them."

"Even if we know what weapons they use," Ben put in, "one ship could not possibly turn the tide. Once we realize what the current situation is, we can plan what to do next."

"Besides," Anita said, "for pure self-defense, the laser cannons on the *Exedra* are the most effective weapons available."

"You have a point there," Kate said. "But you've only secured the ship, not yourselves. In my profession we're told that the chain is only as strong as its weakest link—namely, the individual. I'm still worried about the lack of hand weapons!"

"I am putting the finishing touches on the calculations," Aristotle called over the ship's communicator.

"Better get to the bridge." Tom grinned at the other three. "We're almost ready for takeoff into null-space!"

A few minutes later he sat down in the pilot's couch and forced himself to think carefully, going over the entire jump process as he understood it. He could not afford to make a single mistake.

The distance the ship would travel and exactly where in the universe it would reemerge had to do with the curvature of space-time. Ben and Aristotle had worked out the immensely complex mathematics involved in fourth-dimensional relationships.

But no one, not even Tom or his father, was absolutely certain of the results.

In null-space, according to Skree scientists, everything was reversed. A black hole would be a white hole. A whirlpool, instead of sucking everything in, would be a vast outpouring of energy. Stars and planets became magnetic opposites. Rather than pulling each other by their gravitational forces, they repelled each other.

The computer was programed to enter the ship into null-space in a certain direction at a particular time and place. They would then pop out at another point. One of the unknown factors was the time it would actually take.

From Tom's calculations, the time in the void had little or nothing to do with how far they would travel. A long distance in real space might translate into a short time in null-space and vice versa.

Tom was fairly confident that they had figured out how the instruments would react to the reversed influences of null-space. To be sure, they had installed a duplicate set of sensors which would operate during their time in the void.

The young inventor satisfied himself that the

bridge and its occupants were secure. Then he looked at Ben.

"Let's get on with it," the computer tech said somewhat nervously.

Tom punched the coded message into the computer.

A split second later, space, as human beings knew it, simply ceased to exist.

Chapter Seven

Tom felt as though he were looking through a photographic negative. Everything was reversed and his brain was having a hard time accepting the changes.

His head hurt. His eyes hurt. His lungs burned.

He struggled to see the ship's chronometer, but he could not read it clearly. It appeared to be frozen, anyway. *Time dilation?* he thought groggily.

He did not know how much longer he would be able to endure the void without getting sick.

Suddenly it was over.

Ben gasped, "We're through!"

"Oh, my aching head!" Anita said weakly.

All around him, Tom heard the sounds of his friends relaxing—no—luxuriating with relief. It was a celebration of continued life.

The drive had worked. At least they were in normal space again and they were alive.

But the young inventor knew he could not relax. They were not in the Sol system any longer, that much he could tell by looking out the port at the stars. The orientation of the ship's navigational computer needed to be checked immediately.

"What's our starlock, Aristotle?" he called to the robot, who, like his creator, had not ceased working.

"The computer is staying with Canopus as the lock star. I agree with its choice. Sunlock is Alpha Centauri A."

"We're right on the button, then," said Tom excitedly and everyone cheered in delight.

"What does all that mean?" Kate asked. "Are we lost already?"

Tom heard a slight edge of fear in the girl's voice and he quickly spoke to reassure her. "The navigational computer keeps us on course, a process known as tri-axis navigation or triangulation. The Star Tracker sensors choose a bright star by sensing its brightness electro-optically. That's what we call a starlock. I was worried because the brightness identification data in the computer memory banks are based on readings taken by Earth telescopes. That might have confused and disoriented the Star Tracker as it searched for Canopus here but, fortunately, it didn't."

"Sunlock is the other axis," Ben continued. "The sunlock sensors work just like the Star Tracker sensors, only they use the sun of the solar system we're trying to navigate in as the reference point. With those two knowns the computer determines the parallax and that's how we know where we are."

"That doesn't sound complicated," Kate said.

Tom smiled. "This is a triple-star system, however, so the sunlock sensors have to be aimed very carefully. The two main suns, called Alpha Centauri A and B, are being orbited by a third star, Proxima Centauri."

"That's going to make for some crazy and very dangerous solar flare conditions," Ben put in thoughtfully. "I'm going to work on that problem."

"Good," Tom said. "The experimental hull

coating on *Exedra* that was donated to our cause by my father is supposed to stand up under peak radiation conditions. It was tested in every conceivable situation the techs could think of, and it kept the radiation levels within the safety margins. Still, the *Exedra* is the first ship to be coated by it."

"In other words, the material has never been tested in the field," Anita said. "That doesn't make me feel very secure!"

"How reliable is the information that Aristotle has on the Skree?" Kate asked.

"There's no way of knowing," Tom replied. "The probe that he got it from was working when we found it on Io, but the poor thing had gone crazy from being trapped in volcanic rock. The pressure of knowing the importance of its mission and not being able to carry it out was too much for the alien. But at least some of that information was good enough to get all of us here safely."

"And the Skree planet is Earthlike?" Kate asked.

"Yes," Aristotle spoke up. "I predict that there will be subtle changes in the structure of many plants and animals, but then there are some plants and animals on Earth that look very alien.

I am excited by the prospect of mapping and cataloging a world where dinosaurlike creatures may have survived, for example."

"What?" said Ben, shocked. "That sounds crazy!"

"It is all theoretical, you understand," the robot declared, "but it is a scientific fact that the dinosaurs on Earth flourished until sometime in the Cretaceous Period of the Mesozoic Era, approximately 100 million years ago. Then, suddenly, they became extinct. The fossil content of that strata shows that the Earth was subjected to a mysterious catastrophe which is now believed to be the result of the effects of a supernova reaching the planet."

"This must have disturbed the atmosphere, allowing great amounts of ultraviolet light to reach life on the surface," Tom put in.

"That is correct. The planet's axis of inclination may have been changed as well," Aristotle went on. "There was a sudden drop in Earth temperature and a change in the vegetation as a result. The Ice Age followed."

Ben broke in. "Are you saying that if no such disaster befell the planets in the Alpha Centauri system, their dinosaurs may still exist?"

"Yes, Ben."

"That sounds like a good plot for a book,"

Anita said. "I'm not saying it couldn't happen, though."

"I'd like to add something to Aristotle's theory," Kate said. "The dinosaurs became extinct on Earth because they couldn't adapt to the new climate. One of the reasons human beings have been able to survive and evolve is because we adapt very well to change. That's why we're in space and that's why we'll continue to move outward from our planet unless we're totally wiped out by another form of life for whose weapons we have no defense. We can handle catastrophes. Extermination is something else."

"What are the capabilities of the enemy we'll be facing?" Anita asked.

Aristotle answered at once. "According to my information, the Skree began exploring and colonizing the uninhabited worlds in their system as soon as they developed rocket flight. Later, when they invented what they called their space drive, they moved farther outward. They had the misfortune to stumble on Tharcon, a world inhabited by a savage race which the Skree call the Chutans. The Skree escaped the encounter, but not before they had lost several of their ships. With those ships, the Chutans ruthlessly and methodically proceeded to conquer and enslave their planetary neighbors."

"Why is it everything you tell us today sounds like a bad movie, Aristotle?" Ben asked with a grin.

The robot did not comment on the remark. Instead, he went on, "As fate would have it, some centuries later, the Skree bumped into the Chutans again. Only this time, it was *stardrive* ships that the Chutans stole, ships with a drive similar to the one we put together for the *Exedra*."

"Except that we had to improvise where the Skree probe's data was missing," Ben put in. "So our stardrive isn't quite the same."

"If these Chutans are as aggressive as you say they are, we must never let them discover the location of Earth," Kate said solemnly. "No matter what it costs, we have to pledge that."

Anita sighed. "You make it sound so final."

"It is, in a way," Kate said. Then she chuckled softly, "I can't help it if I think like a soldier."

Tom had been quiet during the discussion among his friends, feeling responsible for all the frightening things that they now had to think about. Inadvertently, his eyes drifted to the monitors in front of him and, for a split-second, he froze. His brain refused to register what his eyes saw.

"A ship," Tom said almost inaudibly.

"Did you say something?" asked Ben, turning toward him.

"A ship!"

Ben followed Tom's pointing finger and stared open-mouthed. "That's the picture from the fixed-position starboard camera with the 2,000-millimeter lens," he said excitedly. "They're still pretty far away, so we have a little time."

"Put the wide-angle roving camera on it, too," said Tom, recovering from his shock at seeing an alien spaceship. "And activate the cameras to record all of this."

"What's going on?" Anita asked. The beautiful redhead literally swam across the weightless bridge and steadied herself on the back of Tom's couch. She gasped when she saw the image on the monitor. Kate came up beside her. If the Indian girl had any fears upon seeing the vessel, she did not voice them. Instead, she watched the monitor in silence.

The first alien starship!

"It's what we've been expecting to see, and yet all my insides have suddenly turned to jelly," Ben said.

"What if it's not a Skree ship?" Anita asked. "It looks so big and we're so small. What are we going to do?"

Tom understood her apprehension. Something deep inside him wanted to run, too. He fought the fear of the unknown with reason. "Any move we make could be interpreted as hostile by the aliens—whoever they are!" he declared. "We'll just have to sit and chew our fingernails until they get here. Aristotle, send a message of friendship in both English and Skree!"

"Wise move," Kate whispered.

A tense silence fell on the bridge of the *Exedra* as Tom and his friends watched the monitor. Aristotle was beaming his message to the aliens through the ship's communications channels and they all hoped fervently that it was a Skree ship approaching.

"I'll place the picture from the camera with the wide-angle lens on the main monitor," Ben said. "And I'll put on the magnification filters, too. There'll be some distortion, but at least we'll be able to see the ship in more detail. Then maybe we'll know whom it belongs to, the Skree—or the Chutans!"

The picture on the monitor jumped and now they could see the entire alien ship. The magnification filters on the wide-angle lens made the edges blurry and the delicate, spidery craft appeared to float as if it were suspended in the universe.

"I would say that it's a Skree ship," Tom said, relief evident in his voice. "It has the same design characteristics that were on the probe's exoskeleton."

"It looks like a big, golden spider with its legs folded up under it," Anita declared. "I saw a spider like that on a rosebush when I was Earthside one time. Yech!"

"Somehow, I expected the alien ship to look more like one of ours," Kate put in. "I don't know why. I guess my mind wasn't prepared to accept something so different."

"No, your assumption that the Skree ships would be like ours is valid, Kate," said Aristotle. "The Skree live in the same universe that we do and physical laws are physical laws. They have to build their ships to withstand much the same conditions as ours. I see instruments on the hull of that ship similar to those on the *Exedra*. But I can also see beyond the stylistic aspects of its construction and perceive the machine much clearer than a human can. It takes a computer to know a computer."

"Have the Skree responded to our friendship signals yet, Aristotle?" Tom asked anxiously.

"I am receiving only static," the robot answered. "The probe was familiar with radio communication, so it is not that—wait! They have found our frequency, Tom! They—"

"Yes? What is it?" Tom asked eagerly. His throat felt very dry and, as he watched the monitor, he already knew what Aristotle's next words would be. The alien ship was pointing a very long and lethal-looking stinger at the *Exedra!*

"They want us to follow them into their system," the robot said. "If we deviate so much as one second of arc from the course they set, they will destroy us! We are prisoners!"

Chapter Eight

"Aristotle, didn't they get our message of friendship?" Tom asked.

"Apparently they received it, but they do not trust us. Instead, they are repeating their instructions," the robot replied.

"Can't we switch on the video communicators?" asked Ben anxiously. "I don't like the idea of being a prisoner so soon. Besides, if we could talk with them face to face—"

Aristotle cut the young man off. "They are jamming all our signals except the first friendship message. I would strongly urge that we follow the ship wherever it wants to take us. We can use the intervening time to run some tests on the environment and perhaps learn more about the Skree. That way we can eventually manage to communicate with them on a more equal basis."

"Besides," Kate added ruefully, "I doubt that we have much choice at this point!"

"Okay, Aristotle," Tom said. "Signal the ship that we will follow. But keep telling them we are friendly. And try to get the captain of that ship to answer my greetings."

The young inventor turned to his companions. "Until we hear more from the alien ship, let's evaluate our surroundings. Just stay on your toes. The first thing to do is to strap on our translator-teachers. It should be worn at all times from now on."

Kate looked puzzled, so Tom explained how the tiny black squares worked. "Unfortunately, we have only three of them. I'll make up another one for you, but until then you'd better just stay close to one of us."

Tom scanned the computer printouts from the experiments Aristotle had begun conducting.

"The planets of the Alpha Centauri A system—the Skra system—bear a remarkable resemblance to the planets in our solar system," the young inventor deduced.

"Yes," the robot agreed. "In comparing the gross characteristics, I find the Skra planets fall nicely into two different groups, just as ours do. The three outer planets might even be called Jovian types. They are the farthest from their sun. They are all large and formed of the lighter elements and they have many satellites. That is just like the planets farthest from our Sun."

The mechanoid double-checked some data on a viewscreen. "The planet that we are approaching is a terrestrial type. It is smaller, made of rocks and metals, and the period of rotation about its sun is quite slow. I have only been able to detect one moon. That is a fascinating coincidence."

"I guess so," said Tom.

"You sound less than excited about it," said the robot, fixing its camera eyes on Tom.

"Ordinarily I'd be jumping up and down at the idea of studying an alien star system, but doing it while a prisoner of the Skree takes the fun out of it," Tom declared.

"You can mope about it if you want to, but I'm furious!" said Ben Walking Eagle, floating up from his copilot's couch. "They delegate a probe to another star system asking for help, we come in answer to their call, and then we're treated like an enemy!"

"Look at it from their side, though," Tom suggested. "They sent out probes at random, in every direction, knowing that a certain percentage of them would probably end up in systems inhabited by beings just as nasty and savage as the Chutans. They must have figured that the rewards would outweigh the risks, but they're not taking any chances and that's wise of them. If the situation were reversed, I would be acting the same way the Skree are. Just because we're here doesn't mean we're here to *help!* We've got to prove our intentions. I don't know how we're going to do that, though."

"I wish I could get them on ship-to-ship video," said Ben.

"No way." Aristotle told him. "They are continuing to block our video signals."

Tom took a deep breath and let it out noisily. That was always an indication that he had made an important decision. Both Aristotle and Ben looked at him expectantly.

"I'm tired of sitting here in isolation! That's what bothers me the most. Aristotle, change our message of friendship to one demanding I be allowed to speak to the captain of that Skree ship!" Tom ordered.

"Is that wise?" Anita asked, pulling herself onto the bridge.

Kate One Star, who was right behind her, quickly added, "The Skree threats of immediate destruction don't appear to be empty!"

"If they're as advanced as we think they are, they're not going to destroy us for demanding to talk to them." Tom grinned for a moment. "I think they might even be more frightened of us than we are of them!"

The young inventor touched the translator-teacher unit hanging from a chain around his neck, but then shook his head. "No, I'm going to put this on the ship's com," he said, keying the bridge microphone.

"This is Tom Swift of the starship *Exedra* calling the Skree vessel . . ."

"*Sword of Death,*" said Aristotle quickly.

". . . *Sword of Death,*" finished Tom.

"That translates into one Skree word," whispered Anita.

Ben chuckled. "*Exedra* translates into ten words in Skree: 'place where beings of knowledge go to enlighten one another.' I think they'll want to learn the name, *Exedra,* for economy's sake!"

Tom motioned excitedly, cutting off the whispering laughter of his friends.

"*EX . . . edra,*" said a voice, speaking slowly. "I am Mok N'Ghai, Commander of the warship *Sword of Death.* Speak, intruder!"

"Intruder!" said Tom. "We're here as a result of a message we received from your probe—

Aracta. Surely you must have been expecting us or somebody like us!"

"We did not receive the required signal of your arrival," the voice responded slowly.

"By the time we were able to understand the message, the probe's thought processes had deteriorated," said Tom. "We are lucky to have made it to the Skra system at all!"

"Skra?" asked the alien. Tom sat back in his chair, stunned by what sounded like laughter from the Skree commander.

"I don't understand," said Tom.

"I shall have to consult with my officers," was the alien's only response.

"The transmission has been cut," said Aristotle. "Something you said amused him greatly."

"An alien being with a sense of humor can't be all bad," Anita commented.

"Commander Swift." The voice of Mok N'Ghai boomed from the speakers again. "You could only have learned your archaic reference to our sun from one of our probes. This substantiates what you said previously about Aracta, who was sent to galactic sector F. In our mythology, Skra was the ancient giver of life and light. Skranipor, the Earth Mother, was his sister."

"Sun worship," said Tom. "Early civilizations

on our planet had that, too, except that each culture's version differed slightly."

"I do not understand," said the alien. "You are from a planet of many cultures?"

"Be very careful," Anita advised. "I sense that the alien is confused on an issue that is of vital importance to the Skree. You may be walking on eggs here. Better change the subject, if you can, until we know more about the Skree."

Tom nodded. "Can you tell us more about the war you're fighting?" he asked the alien commander.

"I do not have the authority to do that. The Supreme High Council will enlighten you if they deem you worthy. When is the rest of your fleet arriving?"

"They're not," said Tom.

"I do not understand," said Mok N'Ghai.

"There's just us," Tom said, feeling uncomfortable all of a sudden. He turned to his friends and whispered, "I think I said too much!"

"Then your people must have placed their most powerful weapons in your ship," the alien boomed.

"Not exactly," said Tom. "A lot of people didn't want us to come here at all. We humans have a hard time agreeing on anything."

"You call yourselves humans? You said there were many cultures on your planet."

"They are all humans, just different kinds," Tom explained.

"I do not understand," the Skree commander said.

"I am not surprised," said Tom, feeling frustrated. "If you could see us right now, you'd understand what I was saying!"

"It is most unfortunate, but I am told our visual communication systems are not compatible."

Tom looked at Aristotle who gave a good imitation of a shrug. Tom decided not to press the point.

"Since you now know we come in friendship, perhaps you could withdraw the restrictions on our ship," the young man suggested. "Must we continue to be regarded as prisoners?"

"You are prisoners until the Supreme High Command decides otherwise!" the Skree officer retorted sharply and Tom was shaken by the vehemence in his voice.

"Whew, I guess that's that!" Ben said.

Tom decided it would be wise to reestablish a friendlier line of conversation. "You said that Skranipor was the ancient name for the Earth

Mother figure in your mythology. What is the name of your planet, then?"

"Kosanth."

The young inventor shook his head in amazement. "We didn't get the complete message from Aracta. We didn't get the drive; we didn't even get the right information! It's a wonder we're here at all!"

"The error was probably mine," said Aristotle.

Tom opened his mouth to protest, but the ship's alarm cut him off.

"Ships at twelve o'clock high!" Ben shouted.

"It is a Chutan patrol—and in this sector, too!" said the commander. Mok N'Ghai sounded more insulted than alarmed. "They are getting bolder by the year. Commander Swift, you would do well to stay out of this skirmish. The Chutans and their allies have many devious ways of fighting which you should observe before you engage in them. I must sign off now."

The communication was severed abruptly.

"We can't just sit here!" Kate One Star shouted in frustration.

"Some of those ships look like Skree vessels!" Tom commented, scanning the monitors. The five approaching craft were small and seemed to be much more maneuverable than the large

Skree warship. But they were similar in appearance. The raiders were spreading out for their attack.

"I am picking up the Chutans' communications," said Aristotle.

"Great!" said Tom. "Work on recording as much of the vocabulary as possible. Knowing their language will help us!"

"It is closer to ours in sound than the Skree tongue," the robot stated. "Listen."

Tom and his friends heard the excited aliens talking over the ship's com. The computer was beginning to supply a crude translation which Tom knew would improve rapidly. Aristotle had been right. Skree words were composed of hard consonants, clicks, pops, and glottal stops, whereas the Chutan tongue sounded more fluid. Vowel sounds were prominent and the tones were generally more rounded.

"Now that the ships are closer, I can see that two of them *are* Skree ships," Ben said. "But they certainly don't look new! Two of the raiders are definitely not of Skree design and the fifth one is a mechanic's nightmare. I don't know how it even keeps up with the others!"

Tom had to agree with his friend. The Skree warships seemed to be made of burnished golden metal, but the captured Skree fighters looked bruised and battered. One was missing two of its leg-like structures and the other had a crude patch on its hull. The ship Ben had called a mechanic's nightmare was made up of pieces of several other craft and definitely had a hard time keeping in formation with the rest.

"It seems odd that a group this ragged would mount a major campaign against an obviously superior military force without good reason!" Kate said thoughtfully.

"There is something else that adds to the mystery surrounding this adventure," Aristotle added. "The Chutan attack force keeps using one word over and over again in reference to the Skree. You may think I am merely trying to make a linguistic point, but the unsettling thing is that it is a Skree word. The computer keeps translating it into English the same way each time—bug. The connotation is definitely derogatory."

There was a moment of shocked silence before Tom laughed. "Come on," he said. "We expected to meet alien beings when we got here. It's silly and terribly naive of us to suppose that they would use the same insults as we do!"

"Yes, but *bugs!*" Anita shuddered.

"Remember, the term is relative," Ben explained. "When we see the Skree, they may look like insects! The computer's ability to make subtle value judgments is based on very limited data input right now."

"Let's keep an open mind," said Tom. "We came here intending to be allies of the Skree. The *Sword of Death* has no fighter escort and I think we should—"

The young man's words were cut off by a violent explosion! The *Exedra* shuddered and bucked, throwing the young people to the deck. The lights on the control panel began to blink and an ear-splitting alarm sounded.

"Tom!" Kate gasped in dismay. "We are being attacked by the Chutans!"

Chapter Nine

"Stand by for evasive maneuvers!" Tom shouted. "Please get to your stations and strap in immediately!"

Anita and Kate, assigned to handle the *Exedra*'s rear defenses, swam rapidly to the back of the ship. Ben swung himself into the copilot's couch. Aristotle remained at the navigation station.

"We're ready," came Anita's voice over the ship's com a few moments later. "I'm plugged into the computer and we're switching to tactical."

"Acknowledged," said Tom. "We're switching to tactical also."

Ben had investigated the battle computer's

subroutines after the close encounter with the *Roxanne* outside *New America.*

One of the most valuable discoveries had been the computer's tactical mode. With it, certain CRT screens could be used to display tactical information in three-color animation. That way, the crew of the *Exedra* was able to see space divided into quadrants or look at the deployment of any attack force in several different ways.

The fact that Anita had plugged the computer in her artificial leg into the battle computer also meant that the *Exedra*'s rear defenses would be hard to break through.

Ben smiled weakly at Tom. "I guess I finally get to play Buck Rogers instead of being just a computer jockey!"

Tom laughed. "I'm going to put us in a better fighting position. The *Sword of Death* is blocking us right now." He pulled back on the acceleration control and felt the familiar g-force push him back into his couch. The *Exedra* slipped quickly out from behind the large Skree warship.

The young inventor keyed the radio microphone and called Mok N'Ghai. "We're sitting ducks here, Commander. Since the Chutans shot at us, we're joining the fight and will assist you as best we can. Over and out."

"*Exedra!* How did you move so fast? Your spacedrive is better than ours!" The commander sounded impressed. "None of our planetary ships even begin to match the speed of your vessel. We are honored to have you fighting on our side!"

He signed off and Tom grinned. "Let's get behind the Chutan formation and harass them from behind. That's where we can do the most good!"

"They're on to our strategy," Ben stated, looking from the tactical screens to a camera monitor. The ship with the patched hull had broken formation and was pursuing the *Exedra.*

Suddenly several short bursts of ruby light shot from the stinger of the battered fighter. Tom put his ship into a backward loop and the deadly beams streaked past to dissipate in space a moment later.

"Good move!" Kate's voice complimented Tom on the com.

The loop had put the *Exedra* on the other side of their adversary and Tom sensed the momentary confusion of the pilot. The Chutan brought his vessel around to face the *Exedra* too late. Ben had already fired a laser cannon and, as Tom put their ship into a steep climb, the beam struck the fighter. The enemy craft collapsed into itself, then broke apart. On the tactical screens, one dot winked out.

"One for our side!" Tom cried triumphantly.

"The mechanic's nightmare is definitely out of the fight," Ben agreed.

Tom saw another fighter, this one of unknown origin, break away from the attack formation on the *Sword of Death* and head toward the *Exedra*. At the same time, one more enemy dot winked out on the tactical screens.

"Score one for the *Sword of Death!*" Ben chortled.

"The remaining fighters engaged in a battle with the Skree warship are suggesting retreat," Aristotle reported. "Interesting. There is an argument going on between them about us."

"Let's see if our attacker falls for the same trick as the mechanic's nightmare," Tom said as he put the *Exedra* into a steep climb ending in a backward loop.

"Nope." Ben watched the screens closely. "That ship has a good pilot. The only problem is, he doesn't have a good ship! It's not fast enough."

An indicator light on the control panel began blinking. Tom knew it was the signal that the *Ex-*

edra's rear cannons were being fired. Less than a second later, the pursuing dot winked out.

"One of the last two fighters is taking off," Ben announced. "Shall we pursue?"

"No, let him—" Tom started to reply when the remaining dot suddenly went into a spin.

"The *Sword of Death* finished him off!" Anita shouted over the com. "We saw it happen!"

Tom keyed the microphone. "*Sword of Death,* the ship you just hit is veering—he seems to be disabled. I'm going to investigate and offer aid. Are you equipped to take prisoners on board your ship?"

"Commander Swift—"

The enemy fighter exploded without warning.

"They self-destructed!" exclaimed Ben.

"Commander Swift, Chutan fighter pilots *never* surrender!" Mok N'Ghai said. "Unfortunately, one of them got away. Well, I hope you will permit us to look at your spacedrive when we get to Kosanth. I think there is much that the Skree can learn from humans, and your extraordinary conduct here will be on my report to the High Council."

"Thank you, Commander," Tom said. "Now, if you will excuse me, my crew and I would like to rest for a while so that we will be able to fully answer all the questions that your High Council might ask us."

"Of course," Mok N'Ghai agreed. "I will keep you informed. Though technically you must remain prisoners, your aid here is sufficient reason for us to relax our restrictions."

The young inventor switched off the microphone. Suddenly he felt very tired and for the first time in many hours, he allowed himself the luxury of leaning back in his couch. He turned his head and looked at Ben, who was glancing out the port.

"Why do Chutan fighter pilots fear capture so much that they self-destruct in order to avoid it?" Tom asked his friend.

"That's usually done when capture is more grisly than death," Kate said, pulling herself onto the bridge.

"That was going to be my answer, too," Ben agreed.

"Granted, it's sometimes a matter of a culture's battle code," Kate went on, "but most of the time it's to avoid torture."

"So you think the Skree torture their prisoners?" Tom asked. "I didn't get that impression from talking to Mok N'Ghai."

"Maybe the Chutans are crazy fanatics," Ben suggested. "Or else *they* torture their prisoners and expect everyone else to follow that code."

Tom took a deep breath. He was worried about all the inconsistencies they had discovered regarding the mysterious aliens.

"Dinnertime!" came Anita's voice over the com.

"Oh, no!" exclaimed Ben. "It's Red's night in the galley!"

"I heard that, Benjamin Franklin Stumbling Eagle, and I'm going to ignore it!" said Anita. "Tonight's bill of fare includes puréed prime rib au jus, puréed spinach in butter sauce, and puréed fresh garden salad!"

"I hope we get to Kosanth in a hurry," said Tom. "No offense to your cooking, Anita, but I hate meals in space!"

"Too bad we won't arrive in time to save ourselves from tonight's repast," Ben teased.

"Just for that, you're going to *wear* your spinach!" Anita retorted.

Four hours later, Tom sat strapped into his couch, feeling useless while the computer took care of the final stages of touchdown. "I hate hard landings," he said through his clenched teeth, which were chattering from the tremendous vibration caused by the solid-fuel rockets laboring to make the landing as smooth as possible. Despite all the effort, Tom knew he would

have a sore back for some time from the rough-
ness of their touchdown.

"Contact!" shouted Ben, next to him.

Tom gasped as he felt the weight of the planet
Kosanth pulling him down. His muscles and
bones ached in protest. Had they been weightless *that* long? Tom was thankful for the isomet-
ric exercises he had forced everyone to do
during each waking period they had spent in
deep space. Still, they would be quite sore for a
while!

"All clear," Ben announced. "I'm shutting
down the fuel systems."

Tom heard grunts and groans from his friends
as they unstrapped themselves and stood up. He
went to the largest side port and looked out. Kosanth was so incredibly flat that the horizon
seemed almost artificial.

"Commander Swift, allow me, please, to wel-
come you and your crew to Kosanth." Mok
N'Ghai's voice sounded excitedly over the *Exedra*'s com. "A shuttle craft will soon arrive at the
base of your ship to take you to the Council. I
look forward to meeting you there."

"Thank you, Commander. We look forward to
the occasion," Tom replied politely.

A short distance away, Tom saw the shuttle
craft against a soft pastel sky that was quite dra-

matic. Moving closer, Tom looked right and left through the port. The Kosanth spaceport was huge and crowded with clusters of buildings.

The *Exedra* was so high above ground level that Tom had to squint his eyes to see tiny figures running toward the shuttle craft.

Anita pushed in next to him. "From up here the Skree look pretty normal," she observed. "They walk on two legs, but those long robes hide a lot. Also, since we're watching from above, we can't get the proper perspective."

"They're rather dark," Tom said, "a kind of chestnut color."

Ben spoke up. "Atmosphere checks out okay. It has the proper oxygen-nitrogen mix for us, anyway. There are some variations on the minor gases, but we won't need artificial aids to breathe."

"They're waiting for us," Tom said, watching a crowd build up around the base of the ship.

"I hope we don't disappoint them," Kate declared. "I suggest we take some of the silver, in case etiquette requires that we bring them gifts. On the other hand, it wouldn't hurt if we took the hand weapons, the knife, and the matches, too. One never knows!" She went off to get the items she had mentioned.

Tom was still looking out the port. "Apparently Commander N'Ghai is the hero of the day!" he said.

"Or heroine," Anita added.

Tom grinned ruefully. Then he activated the airlock. "Well, it's time for man to meet another life form!" With that, he stepped out. The others followed.

The young inventor knew at once that something was wrong. All of a sudden there was complete silence. A soft wind blew between the starships and ruffled the robes of the Skree. Then came whispers from the crowd. Tom adjusted his T-T unit and heard the voices through the translator:

"Chutans! They're Chutans!"

One of the figures in the foreground who wore an elaborately embroidered robe pointed angrily at the visitors from Earth. The T-T unit crackled with his spoken words.

"Seize them and the traitor who brought them here!"

Tom stared at the accuser in shock and surprise. The Skree's hood had fallen back and they could clearly see the head and face of their accuser.

All of them tensed, gaping in stunned surprise.

"They're insects!" Anita cried out.

"Anita!" snapped Tom. "Don't use that word!"

But Anita didn't listen. In a ringing voice of disgust she sputtered, "They're bugs! Huge *bugs!*"

Chapter Ten

A cry of anger went up from the crowd at Anita's remark.

The four young people and Aristotle were instantly surrounded by a group of figures who were obviously guards. They carried weapons with authority and obviously had used them many times.

"I don't believe this!" Ben exclaimed angrily. "A great historical occasion is turning into a lynching party!"

The Skree guard who had come up behind the young computer tech gave him a shove. "Silence, Chutan dog!"

"Cool it!" Tom whispered to his friend. "Save your energy for a time when we might need it."

Ben nodded stiffly.

Tom could tell that his friend was more agitated than frightened by their capture. For that matter, the situation had not infected any of them with a sense of impending doom. No one could believe that the Skree were capable of disregarding the help they had received and would judge the humans only by their unfortunate resemblance to their enemy.

They were being marched away from the spaceport toward a large building some distance away. No shuttle for prisoners, Tom thought wryly. Now we have to walk!

Soon they were joined by another group.

"Tom!" Anita whispered excitedly. "I believe one of those creatures is Commander Mok N'Ghai. That's what one guard told another one."

"But why would he be a prisoner? He just defended his planet against the Chutans!" Ben put in.

"Obviously, the bad news of our presence cancelled out the good news of winning the battle," Tom guessed. "I hope we'll be able to explain the situation to someone in authority soon!"

"First City!" one of the guards said proudly, pointing into the distance. Tom tried to talk to him further, but he refused to say anything more.

When they got closer to First City, they saw a three-tiered tower with landscaping and what were apparently residential areas above ground. From the movement around entrances leading into the ground, Tom suspected most of the city was underground.

"This way!" the guard commanded and they were led to a tunnel. Though Tom tried to keep his sense of direction intact, he soon lost track of the numerous twists and turns they made. However, the underground city through which they were led was perhaps the most beautiful he had ever seen.

"Everything looks as though it had flowed into existence rather than having been constructed with tools," Anita pointed out. "There are no sharp corners or visible joints."

Tom nodded. He noticed that high, curved archways dominated the architecture. The city had obviously been built of a material that looked like rock but had been liquefied and then molded over a framework. All of First City seemed to have been made from the same substance, shaped by the Skree builders to be in harmony with the environment.

The guards were evidently taking their prisoners to their destination by a little-used route, since few inhabitants of First City were to be seen. Those the humans did encounter appeared to be much like their welcoming committee; they were a chestnut-brown color and wore long flowing robes. Tom guessed the varying degrees of decoration signified their rank or status.

He cast another glance at Mok N'Ghai and the guards. The Skree tended to be several inches taller than his own six feet. They bore a definite resemblance to the insects on Earth, and Tom was not able to distinguish the males from the females. He wondered if it would be an unpardonable sin to ask about such identification. His curiosity would have to wait.

Abruptly the guards halted and opened a door, revealing a cluster of austerely furnished rooms. Tom looked around quickly. To his relief he saw nothing that looked even remotely like an instrument of torture.

"In here!" one of the guards commanded The entire group was herded into a single room.

Once inside, two more guards entered with a large container. "All personal possessions must be surrendered," one of the guards announced, reaching for Anita's necklace.

"No!" the redhead shrieked in terror.

Stunned by the vehemence of Anita's emotion, the guard stepped back.

"Please," Kate said to him. "Let me do it." She removed Anita's necklace and handed it over.

Swiftly the Skree collected watches, jewelry, keys, and everything else the young people had brought with them. As one dropped the articles in the container, the second one recorded them on a tablet he carried.

"When we get out of jail, I suppose we can claim our belongings," Ben muttered in irritation.

"Of course," the Skree with the tablet responded.

When the guards left their prisoners, Tom suddenly realized they had not even looked at Mok N'Ghai.

Time seemed to pass slowly, though it was impossible to tell with any accuracy. No one spoke. There were no windows or light wells on this level of the city. Finally Ben stood up to pace the room.

"Will you please sit down?" Tom mumbled after a while. "I'm getting tired watching you and I need all my energy to think of a way out of this!"

Ben mumbled an apology and sank down on the floor.

"It's all my fault," Anita wailed.

"That is my line," said Aristotle in what Tom guessed to be the robot's attempt at humor.

"I don't know what's the matter with me! I just can't get used to the way the Skree look!" the beautiful redhead whispered. "You know that we don't have insects on *New America* except for cockroaches. I used to have nightmares about them. I would dream that huge horrible bugs were crawling all over me. I could feel their little hairy legs prickling my skin and I saw their soft white bellies pulsating. Their antennae wiggled back and forth constantly and their mandibles moved in and out." Anita opened and closed her hands for emphasis. "I just knew they would eat me if I didn't wake up!"

"Anita," Tom said, but she was not to be stopped.

"Once I was reaching into a kitchen cupboard for a cracker and I accidently touched a cockroach," she continued. "It almost scared me to death. The nightmares were worse after that."

"You guys are the sorriest bunch of space adventurers I've ever seen!" snapped Kate. "If you're through with the self-pity, maybe you'd like to get down to the business of planning what we should do next!"

"That's heartless of you, Kate," Ben said.

"No," Anita said softly. "She's right. I'm letting an old memory cloud my thinking and my judgment. The Skree are hardly the same as the little creatures scurrying around my cupboards at home. I have to remember that and fight my fear with every ounce of intelligence I've got!"

Tom glanced self-consciously toward Mok N'Ghai, who had remained sitting on the floor in one corner of the cell with his back against a wall. Had he heard what Anita said?

The commander returned Tom's glance but gave no indication whether he had understood the conversation. He had not spoken since his arrest at the spaceport and seemed to want nothing to do with the humans. Unlike the officials dressed in long flowing robes, whom Tom had seen at the spaceport, the commander was wearing a shiny black segmented body armor over a long kilt of red material with gold trim. On his feet he wore heavy boots. The uniform almost gave him the appearance of a soldier of ancient Rome.

Tom looked down at his own simple, utilitarian, light-blue jumpsuit and soft-soled sneakers. They were hardly stylish. Anita's green jumpsuit was not much more fashionable than his, but at least it had the advantage of setting off her red hair and large hazel eyes. Ben looked quite handsome in his red and white tie-dyed T-shirt and faded blue jeans, but next to the elegantly dressed Skree, the humans looked shabby.

The young inventor suddenly felt guilty about involving Mok N'Ghai in the trouble that their trip to Alpha Centauri had caused. Tom suspected that they had probably accidently brought about the ruin of the Skree commander's military career, even though the alien seemed to be taking his misfortune with great dignity and silent courage. Tom decided that he would try to communicate with the commander in an effort to get to know him better.

"Commander N'Ghai, surely the High Council won't hold this against you!" he began. "Our space battle with the Chutan raiders should be proof of our intentions. It speaks for itself. It's just a coincidence that we resemble your enemies."

The Skree officer stirred. "It is hard for me to put aside old hatreds when I look at your forms, just as it is hard for you. But I saw how you fought the Chutans and that means something. Alas, I am only the commander of a warship and I doubt that when the Council finishes with me I will even be that.

"Soon after the battle, I beamed a full report down to them, so they knew of your exploits and heroic conduct before your ship landed. Yet, when they saw you, it made no difference," he said thoughtfully. "This is not a good sign."

"Is there nothing we can do to convince them we are not their enemies?" Kate asked.

"There are many things about you that do not fit into what we know of the Chutans," the Skree continued. "This may save you."

Mok N'Ghai rose gracefully to his feet and walked over to Anita. Much to everyone's astonishment, he reached out and touched her hair. Tom held his breath, but Anita did not flinch or back away.

"This one's hair is the color of flames. Is it a cosmetic trick or do humans have this coloring naturally?" the commander asked.

"Anita's hair is rare among humans, but it is natural," said Tom.

"I think it is quite beautiful," said the Skree. The comment caught Tom totally off guard and he stared at the alien in shocked surprise. Anita seemed puzzled, then her expression changed to comprehension.

"Do we humans all look alike to you?" she asked the commander. "You just made a remarkable comparison about us."

Mok N'Ghai was silent for a moment. Then he said, "No, you do not look quite the same to me.

But then, you yourselves told me that there were different types of humans. I was prepared for more drastic differences than you actually exhibit. Also, I think I am more used to aliens than you are, since I have been to many planets inhabited by intelligent but non-Skree life forms. If I understand you correctly, this is your species' first encounter with a race different from your own."

"I feel like a hick," said Tom. "I am ashamed to admit you're right, Mok N'Ghai, and my behavior toward you and your people has been less than sophisticated because of that. You must be forming terrible opinions about us!"

"On the contrary. I am fascinated by all of the contradictions I've observed in your nature," said the Skree. "It is true, you do exhibit a great deal of naiveté, and yet you also have the intelligence and technical sophistication to build an interstellar driveship."

Suddenly they heard shuffling noises outside the cell. A guard entered with a great flurry. "You will come with me," he announced. "The High Council wishes to examine you at once!"

Chapter Eleven

The Great Hall of the High Council was a vast, airy chamber. Light streamed down from intricately wrought ceiling panels onto the floor, giving the room an expansive, cathedral-like feeling.

In the center stood a huge table made of the same kind of poured stone that the young people had seen throughout First City. Around it sat a number of Skree, apparently the members of the High Council.

The walls of the Great Hall were crowded with spectators and their whispers buzzed in the room. The noise intensified as Tom, his friends, and Mok N'Ghai entered and were ushered to seats. Tom wanted to ask the commander what was going to happen next, but he knew that if Mok N'Ghai's people saw him talking to the humans, it would only confirm their suspicion that he was a traitor. It would be better to wait until they had all been cleared of spy charges.

"Do you notice how the colors of the spectator's robes seem to fall into separate categories?" Kate whispered.

Tom nodded. "And each shade appears in the robes of the High Council. I wonder why one of the councilors is sitting apart. His robe is the same color as Mok N'Ghai's uniform."

"He must be the representative of the military," Kate guessed.

"No, Kate," Aristotle broke in. "From Aracta's data, I can tell you that Skree society is clan oriented. Each of the councilors represents an entire clan."

"I haven't seen one Skree woman since we got here," said Anita. "And don't try to tell me that all the Skree look alike, either. Where are the females?"

"I hope they're not repressed," Kate said. "That always brings out my militant streak!"

"There are no females here now," said the robot. "In Skree society, the female is the nucleus of the clan. Female births are so rare that each clan has only one in a generation. If, by some chance, two females are born—an event so rare it has not happened in twelve generations—a new clan is formed. If anything happens to the female of a clan before another has been born, the clan dies out."

"Goodness gracious," said Anita. "Imagine living in such a society. It would certainly make you feel wanted!"

"The High Councilors you see in this room are merely representatives of the clans," Aristotle went on. "They will debate our situation and vote on a plan of action, but theirs is not the final word. The female of each clan will cast the deciding vote. The reigning queen of the city then makes her decision based on that. There is a problem regarding our situation, however. First City recently lost their queen and the princess is not old enough to make important decisions for the city. It will be up to the High Regent to decide our fate."

"Is that bad?" Ben asked.

"He was the one who had us arrested," Aristotle replied.

"That's bad," mumbled the young computer tech.

"If this were not a time of war, I think you would see more females here," the robot continued. "At the moment, every effort is being made to protect them, so they are heavily guarded."

"Needless to say, you've been monitoring First City's communications," Tom said.

"I hope you do not think it rude of me," Aristotle explained. "You did not ask me to do it and that perhaps makes it like eavesdropping, but I wanted to do something to help. With First City in such a nervous state, it might be difficult for the Skree to think clearly about our fate."

"Thanks, Aristotle," Tom said. "You may have prevented us from making serious blunders here. Was the queen's death related to the war?"

"Yes. Apparently, she was caught outside the city during a Chutan raid and—"

Further conversation was cut off abruptly as all the Skree in the Great Hall rose to their feet. Tom motioned Ben, Anita, Kate, and Aristotle to do the same. Because of the height of the Skree, it was difficult for humans to see, though Tom and Ben managed to catch an occasional glimpse.

"Isn't that the High Regent?" Ben asked when a tall figure, accompanied by a much smaller one, entered the Great Hall.

"Yes. I recognize the robe," Tom whispered.

The Skree official walked through the crowded room with great dignity. Then he turned to face the assembly and bowed deeply from the waist. After he and his companion were seated, everyone else sat down, too.

Tom watched the small Skree next to the High Regent. It must be the princess, he thought. She looked petite next to the others. Smaller by almost two feet, her feet dangled several inches from the floor. From the shape and size of her feet and hands, the only parts of her body not covered by the ornately embroidered, rust-colored robe, Tom concluded that her structure was very delicate.

Her many-faceted eyes were black, like those of the other Skree, but perhaps because the rest of her body appeared so finely boned, her features seemed larger. Tom also noticed that the color of her skin was several shades lighter than chestnut brown.

The High Regent leaned down and whispered something to her that Tom's T-T unit did not pick up. The comment was obviously about the humans because the young princess turned to stare at them and asked in a loud, clear voice, "How do you think they eat, Uncle?"

There was a half-second of hushed silence in the Great Hall. Then some of the Skree began to laugh. Tom felt himself blushing and noticed that the princess was puzzled. She had not meant her question to be cruel and obviously did not understand why the adults found it funny.

All at once Tom decided to like her.

He glanced sideways at Mok N'Ghai and saw that the commander was staring at the floor in front of him, trying hard not to laugh. The alien must have felt Tom's eyes on him because he looked up for a brief moment. The young inventor wished that he were better at interpreting Skree facial expressions. The way and number of times that they moved their razor-sharp mandibles certainly meant something!

The High Regent stood up, and the laughter immediately stopped. He looked at the humans imperiously and asked, "Which one of you is Tom Swift, commander of the starship *Exedra?*"

Tom rose, but did not speak. He was aware that all the Skree were staring at him intently. What he did now would be taken as representative of the entire human race.

"I am Kagh G'Thoa, High Regent for Princess Eln N'Yn. I have read Commander N'Ghai's report of your conduct during the Chutan attack on the *Sword of Death* and I have listened to the accounts of the crew of that vessel. Their stories differ only slightly from the commander's version. However, the fact remains that you who call yourselves humans look disturbingly like our enemies, the Chutans."

"Except for that one," said the princess, pointing to Anita. "Why is she different, Uncle? I have never seen a Chutan with red hair!"

"It is a minor difference," grumbled Kagh G'Thoa.

"I think it is a clever Chutan trick!" a councilor spoke up. "It is some new thing that they are using to get us to lower our defenses!"

There was a chorus of assenting noises, then Kagh G'Thoa raised his hand for silence. "There is a way we can determine the truth of this. Guards, seize the red-haired human and take some of the creature's hair!"

A guard stepped quickly up to Anita, but she was faster. She jumped from her seat, holding her hair against her neck protectively and ran to Tom's side.

"Don't let them cut off my hair!" she cried.

There was a loud rustling sound in the Great Hall and Tom saw that every Skree had some sort of weapon pointed at them.

"Don't worry," he whispered to Anita, "and stay calm!"

He looked squarely at the High Regent with what he hoped was his most convincing expression of sincerity. "I humbly ask the High Council to allow me to take the sample. We humans attach a certain importance to our hair," he said.

There were signs of uncertainty from the crowd, but the High Regent nodded in assent. One of the guards handed Tom a sharp knife and with great care the boy cut off a small lock of Anita's hair. Any wrong twitch of a muscle and he knew that he and his friends would be killed instantly. He made a deliberate show of handing the knife back to the guard, handle first. A Skree messenger took the lock of hair from him and hurried out of the Great Hall.

"We will have that sample analyzed thoroughly," Kagh G'Thoa said. "If we discover any attempt at trickery, it will mean your doom! You may sit down until you are called upon again."

The High Regent's gaze shifted from Tom and Anita to Mok N'Ghai. "Commander, pending the outcome of the lab results and the final decision of this Council, you are being released on your own recognizance. We do this out of respect for your brilliant record of service to our society. You may roam First City at your will. However, you are temporarily stripped of your rank and all privileges associated with it until the fate of the humans is decided. In the meantime, you may join your clansmen, if you wish."

Mok N'Ghai bowed deeply from the waist toward the princess, then, to everyone's obvious surprise, he walked briskly out of the Great Hall.

Kagh G'Thoa gave no indication that Mok N'Ghai's action shocked him. Instead, he turned to the High Councilors. "I now call a recess until the laboratory's findings are announced," he said.

The audience stood and bowed to the princess, then slowly filed out of the Great Hall.

"Commander Swift," Kagh G'Thoa addressed the young inventor. "I also read the report on your truly remarkable ship. You say that you copied it from our design, yet we have no ship like it. I should like you to show me the *Exedra* now. Guards, you will escort the other humans and their robot back to the cell."

Eln N'Yn reached quickly to grab her uncle's robe and the High Regent leaned down while she whispered something in his ear. Tom saw the alien twitch his mandibles in annoyance.

"Alright," he finally said. "The red-haired one is to stay with Commander Swift!"

Tom and Anita followed the princess and Kagh G'Thoa from the Great Hall down the broad avenue to the spaceport at the edge of First City. The princess and her uncle were almost obscured from the young people's view by the vast number of guards surrounding the Skree royalty.

A few of the townspeople stopped to look at the small procession, but most continued about their business.

Tom did not approve of having the *Exedra* inspected by beings holding him and his friends captive. He also felt rather protective of its secrets. But he did not see any way to avoid complying with the High Regent's wishes.

Suddenly he realized he would not mind discussing the *Exedra*'s unique points with Mok N'Ghai. He was both surprised and pleased to recognize his feeling of friendship toward the alien commander.

However, the young inventor knew he would have to be extremely careful. While seeming to comply with the Skrees' wishes, he must find a way out of their hands.

Tom wondered what his father would do as he pressed his entry code into the *Exedra's* hatch mechanism. The entry lights flashed and Tom quickly stepped through into his ship. He turned to the others and beckoned them to follow.

At that instant, an explosion threw the young inventor against the bulkhead, stunning him. He sank limply to the deck, gasping for air, choking on the thick smoke that was billowing from the hatchway. He peered through it, his eyes smarting, and noticed the guard lying unconscious behind the hatch he had opened.

Tom got shakily to his feet and stumbled forward. He found the High Regent sprawled face down on the deck. Apparently he had taken the full force of the blast.

The young inventor kneeled down beside him to search his body for a sign of life when a powerful kick sent him flying. He hit the deck on his back and looked up to see a laser pointed in his face. The hand that held it was humanoid!

"I do not wish to kill you, alien, so be smart and obey me!" the Chutan commanded.

Chapter Twelve

"Get up!" the intruder hissed and kicked Tom again. Then he barked at the soldiers who had followed him into the *Exedra*. "Up there!" he pointed with his free hand in the direction from which Tom had come, but his eyes and laser never left his prisoner.

The soldiers left.

There was a startled shout, sounds of laser beams striking metal, and a horrifying moan. Tom shuddered, imagining what might be happening to Anita and the princess—and to his ship. Would the *Exedra* be able to take off again or had the lasers ruined the controls?

After a few minutes of silence, one Chutan reappeared. "All clear," he reported to Tom's captor who seemed to be in charge of the raiders.

"Move, alien!" The Chutan prodded Tom with the laser gun. The soldier followed him.

"Tom!" Anita cried as he stepped back onto the bridge.

"Are you all right?" he anxiously asked Anita and the princess.

"Shut up!" the soldiers bellowed.

The Chutan who had captured Tom moved to the other side of the bridge, then turned and faced the prisoners. "Good day, dear people," he said with fake politeness. "Allow me to introduce myself. I am Captain Maris Nim of The Leader's Elite Corps." He puffed out his barrel chest and broadened his already wide smile.

He held up a small electronic device and waggled it in Tom's direction. "We would never have been successful without this, Commander Swift. It was built by our allies, the Chimmies, to jam the signal from the Skree's perimeter defense equipment! It works well, no?"

"So that's how you captured City of Star Machines!" Eln N'Yn angrily blurted out. Anita motioned to the princess to be silent. They were hardly in a position to show any defiance.

The captain's smile lost none of its sinister

brilliance. "That is correct, Princess. However, that knowledge will do you no good. You will never have the opportunity to inform your people of it. You are just as valuable to us as the humans. You will remain alive only as long as that value lasts. I would advise you to stretch it out a long time by being cooperative."

Tom, still feeling the effects of the explosion, couldn't help staring at the short, brown-haired Chutan's prominent canine teeth, which were very white and perfectly even. The young inventor wondered if all Chutans smiled constantly. A soldier, standing watch behind his captain, had the same grin.

He shook himself to clear his head. Kagh G"Thoa and his guard were wounded or dead near the hatch. The other guard on the bridge was lying limply in a corner, moving and moaning occasionally. Two members of the Chutan raiding party were also crumpled on the deck, disabled by the guard after they had tried to rush him from the passageway.

Tom feared that Anita, the princess, and he were in big trouble. He looked over at Anita and Eln N'Yn, standing with their backs to the control panel, their arms raised.

Tom felt utterly helpless as he heard the

sounds of an air attack on First City. The captain noticed his expression. "Merely a small diversion for the real purpose of our trip, Commander Swift," he said.

"Which is?" Tom asked.

"Stealing ships," the Chutan replied.

The Chutans seemed satisfied that their prisoners were helpless. They began to explore the bridge, keeping their weapons pointed in the direction of the young people.

Tom considered rushing the soldier who stood nearest him but dismissed it as stupidity when he realized how outnumbered they were.

However, he did allow himself one small ray of hope. He watched the captain's moves carefully and, although Maris Nim tried to hide it, there was something awkward about his examination of the *Exedra's* control systems. It looked as if he were trying to figure out how to launch the ship. Not having much success, he was obviously growing impatient.

With good reason, Tom thought. An air attack could only act as a temporary cover.

Maris Nim and his soldiers actually appeared to be afraid of the *Exedra*. Finally, the captain gave up his pretense of knowing what he was doing. "What is the function of this group of controls?" he asked, pointing to the label affixed to the panel which read, LOWER BAY HATCH.

Tom decided to take a chance. If it paid off, he might have a means of escape for them. If it didn't, he might be guaranteeing their deaths on the spot! He glanced at Anita, who was still plugged into the ship's computer. She had been demonstrating an artful color-graphics program before the attack.

"That is the main computer control," the young inventor said as matter-of-factly as he could. "Why don't you switch it on?"

The alien nodded. "Of course," he said, and pulled down the lever. There was a loud thump from the underside of the ship. The two Chutans suddenly looked as if they were going to bolt from the ship at any moment.

"Up there!" shouted the young inventor, and pointed at a CRT monitor which had suddenly sprung to life. "Sorry about the noise. The thing hasn't worked right since we left Omega Epsilon Gamma Globulin Four!" He blurted out the first authentic-sounding star name that popped into his brain.

The Chutans seemed shaken, but believed Tom's story. He resisted the temptation to wipe his forehead in relief and looked at Anita. She remained silent but slowly spread the first and second fingers of her right hand in a victory sign.

The *Exedra*'s lower hatch, used for dumping garbage, was now open. They would be able to escape through it if they managed to outwit their captors.

"You say that your computer is broken?" Maris Nim asked. "We will have our allies, the Chimmies, repair it when we get to the base. Where is this planet, Omega Epsilon Gamma . . . Gamma . . ."

"Gamma Globulin Four," Tom finished. "It's in the system we call Beta Flangies. I'm sure you have it on your star maps."

"Of course," said the Chutan. "And that is your planet of origin?"

"Oh, yes," Tom said with conviction.

"Do your people have many ships like this one? Not even the Skree have such fine warships," Maris Nim said, trying to fake disinterest.

But Tom knew he was anything but disinterested. The young inventor decided to see how far he could draw out his opponent and get information about the Chutans' war strategy and way of thinking.

"This is the only one," Tom said. "I outfitted this ship as an experiment. When I get back to Omega Epsilon Gamma Globulin, maybe others like it will be constructed."

"You lie!" Maris Nim shouted. With surprising speed, he strode over to Tom and slapped him viciously on the chin. That was as far as he could reach, since the young inventor towered almost two feet above him.

Tom made a show of staggering backward and cowering. The blow had not hurt him much, but his act satisfied Maris Nim that no further demonstration of power was needed.

"I warn you, human, do not lie to me again! We have ways of getting the truth which are very effective! I think your planet has many of these ships. Someday, I should like to go there," Nim said.

"All the more ships for you to steal, eh, Chutan?" the princess said. "That is how these ignorant savages got their mighty fleet, Commander Swift! They are not intelligent enough to build ships of their own!"

Maris Nim angrily whirled at the princess, but to Tom's surprise, he made no move to strike her. Instead, he merely shook a fist at her. "Insolent bug, you try my patience!"

He must want her as a hostage. That's why he doesn't hurt her, Tom thought.

"I'm sorry my people confused humans with these horrible savages," Eln N'Yn whispered to

Anita after Maris Nim had turned his attention back to the ship's controls. "We've been very stupid. I only hope I will be able to right this injustice! You are nothing like the Chutans."

"We don't even look like them," Anita whispered back. "Their skeletal structure is much heavier than ours and they are far shorter than human adults."

Apparently the Chutans had overheard Anita's last comment because they all turned to glare at her.

Tom groaned inwardly. They were up against a force of brutal, scientifically backward beings who smiled all the time.

The captain approached Anita and put his fingers under her chin and raised it slightly. It was a gesture that villains once made in bad movies, Tom thought.

"Maybe we won't kill this one with the others," he gloated. "Our leader might be interested in a new toy!"

"Captain, we must get this ship back to base first," advised one of his soldiers. "The fighters will be stopping their attack soon!"

EEEEEEEEE!

The *Exedra*'s alarm screamed to life so suddenly that even Tom was startled. The effect on the

Chutans was extraordinary. The captain and his soldiers dropped to their knees, terrified.

"What have we done that could make this ship explode, Captain?" one screamed.

"We have offended the gods somehow, Calim, and now we are doomed!" Nim lamented.

At that moment, Mok N'Ghai leaped from the passageway onto the bridge with a needle gun! He landed on his feet in a crouch, and fired at the Chutans. Seconds later, all enemies had collapsed on the deck, unconscious from the gun's tranquilizer-tipped projectiles.

Tom recognized the needle gun as one of the weapons taken from his group when they were arrested. He was glad that the tranquilizing compound worked effectively on Chutan body chemistry.

"Am I glad to see you!" Tom exclaimed.

"It was timely of you to set off the ship's alarm when you did," Mok N'Ghai replied. "It covered the noise of my entrance. How did you know I was out there?"

"I felt your presence," Anita explained. "I'm an empath. A person's—or being's—feelings are like a signature or a fingerprint. No two individuals are exactly alike. After our talk in the prison cell, I stopped blocking your emotions and learned your signature. I sensed you while you were still on the launch surface trying to figure out how to get into the ship. I set off the alarm when I thought the time was right," she finished, and pointed at her computer connection.

"My uncle! Is he—?" cried the princess.

"He is alive, but hurt badly," Mok N'Ghai replied. "The others who came with me have taken him and the guard to the infirmary, Your Highness."

"You took a risk attempting a rescue by yourself," said Tom.

"There was no other way," Mok N'Ghai said. "When the city received the alarm from your ship—"

"Anita again, I'll bet!" Tom laughed.

"When the alarm came, the Chutan air attack had already begun. I was aware of the fact that Eln N'Yn and the High Regent were aboard the *Exedra* and I also remembered that the Chutans knew of the ship. I knew they would try to steal it, putting the princess in grave danger. No one could be spared from the city's defenses, and the rescue of Eln N'Yn might very well be a suicidal mission, anyway. Since I am no longer a commander, I had nothing to lose by trying. I found your weapons and made the attempt."

"The Chutans launched the attack on the city

just to cover their theft of the *Exedra*," said Tom.

"That is typical of them," Mok N'Ghai said. "They must think the ship has strong magic."

At that moment, the Chutan guard stirred.

"That man needs medical attention," said Tom. "My robot, Aristotle, may be able to help."

Mok N'Ghai looked at Tom for a moment, then touched the boy's shoulder. "I am sorry to bring you bad news," he said. "Your friends and your robot have been captured by the Chutans."

Chapter Thirteen

The young inventor stared at the Skree in shocked silence. "Captured? How?"

"A ground force was sent in to take a human in case they needed one to pilot the *Exedra*. The Chutans overpowered the guards as they were taking your friends back to their cell." Mok N'Ghai sighed with frustration. "Since all Skree cities are built on the same basic plan, our enemies knew exactly where to find them. The attack was launched from City of Star Machines which the Chutans hold."

Tom was curious about City of Star Machines, but decided that it would not be appropriate to ask for an explanation at this time.

"Come on," he said instead. "Let's get the wounded taken care of. Then I'm going to find Kate, Ben, and Aristotle!"

"I'll go with you," Eln N'Yn said firmly.

"You cannot go!" gasped Mok N'Ghai in horror. "You are the princess!"

Eln N'Yn stared hard at the commander. "I feel personally responsible for what has happened to the humans and I intend to see my mistake corrected."

"But—" the Skree officer sputtered.

"My uncle is not able to make any decisions, so I am in command now. If I don't go, no one will! Come here," she told him.

The commander obeyed.

"I hereby restore your rank to you and give public gratitude for your bravery this day," the princess intoned formally.

The officer bowed from the waist.

"We've no time to lose," Eln N'Yn said. "Please order some soldiers to guard this ship."

The small group swiftly left the *Exedra* and took the wounded to the nearest hospital in the shuttle. Mok N'Ghai contacted his troops and rejoined the others a few minutes later.

"Where do we start to look?" Tom asked when they were on their way out of the hospital.

Before anyone could answer, Anita suddenly

halted. "Listen!" she said. "I think the Chutans are leaving."

Indeed, the sounds of the air attack were diminishing and a few moments later ceased altogether.

"Hurry!" the princess urged. "This way!" She ushered the group into an underground passage much like the one that had led to their prison cell. This time, however, she took the humans to an armory and gave them weapons.

Eln N'Yn grasped an ornate laser rifle and turned to Anita. "I hereby present you with this weapon in gratitude for your services to the people of Kosanth," she said.

Anita smiled and blinked back tears. "We've come a long way towards understanding each other in the last few hours," she said. "I hope we will have many years to continue learning from each other."

"We will if we can defeat the Chutans," Mok N'Ghai said. "Our next move should be to take a small transport flier and sneak to the outskirts of City of Star Machines. Once we are there, we will be in a position to make our move to free the prisoners."

As if anticipating the question which was forming in Tom's mind, the Skree officer assured him. "After a raid, the Chutans almost always stay within their captured cities. We should be in no danger as long as we wait until nightfall to enter City of Star Machines."

He led the way down the corridor to the hanger where the transport fliers were kept.

After a short trip, the group landed outside the captured city. They moved their flier against a pile of rocks and camouflaged it with dirt and branches. Then they walked toward City of Star Machines.

The brilliant blue sky of Kosanth was deepening and Tom watched in awe as horizontal streaks of fiery red and orange marked the Sun's decent. His backlighting gave an unreal quality to the city's above-ground complex.

The young inventor ducked briefly behind a red sandstone dune to make sure that the needle gun he had brought with him was snug in its holster. Then he checked that the holster was fastened tightly against his leg so it wouldn't slap when he moved. He looked up to see Anita smiling at him, shouldering her new ornate laser rifle.

They walked mostly through wilderness and Tom found that he liked the untouched quality of the terrain. The Skree had never developed a system of roads and superhighways like the ones of Earth. Instead, they used air travel between cities which were surrounded by deserts with colorful, tough vegetation, stretching for miles in every direction.

Tom looked at the sky and guessed that they had about half an hour more to wait before nightfall.

Eln N'Yn stopped and motioned for the group to sit down in a spot protected by rock outcroppings. "This is as far as we can go now," she said. We'll continue after dark."

She pulled a map out of her robe and spread it out in front of her while the others looked over her shoulder. "If we don't have to hide from any Chutan patrols," the princess said, "we'll get into the city very quickly by this route." She traced an imaginary line across the map with her finger.

Tom recognized the symbols on the map and knew it would be tricky. "Isn't there an easier way?" he asked.

Anita punched him jokingly in the arm. "You know, it's a shame *you* weren't captured instead of Ben. He was a boy scout!"

"Thanks!" Tom replied with a hurt expression.

It made Anita laugh.

"You humans have an interesting way of talking to each other," Mok N'Ghai said. "You say one thing, but you mean just the opposite. I find that confusing."

"That's known as sarcasm," Anita chuckled. "We use it at times to tease each other. Our language is structured that way. But it must sound peculiar over our translation units."

Mok N'Ghai reached into the pouch at his side. Much to the surprise of the humans, he brought out the pieces of silverware, the two boxes of matches, and the paring knife that had been taken from them during their arrest in First City.

"I almost forgot these," the alien said. "As we left First City, one of the scientists gave them to me to return to you."

Tom could tell that both aliens were puzzled by the objects.

"Our scientists tried to discover their use," Mok N'Ghai went on. "Except for the small fire-sticks and the knife, they failed. What are the other things for?"

Tom chuckled and held up a fork. "This is an eating utensil. We call it a fork. We cut our food into bite-size pieces with a knife, then we stab the pieces with the fork and carry the food to our mouths."

He picked up another item.

"This is a spoon. It's used for stirring and sipping liquids, like this," Tom said. He pantomimed stirring a bowl of soup and then eating it.

"That is . . . interesting," Mok N'Ghai finally said.

Although the aliens were trying to hide it, they were clearly revolted by the eating customs Tom had described.

The young inventor decided not to pursue the subject further. He put the objects Mok N'Ghai had given him in his jumpsuit pockets, making sure they would not clink together. They might be excess baggage, but then again, they might be handy. He smiled to himself, knowing Kate would have approved.

He wondered where his friends were and what they were doing. He was especially worried about Aristotle's fate at the hands of the Chutans. Perhaps they were forcing the mechanoid to run their war operations!

"Why is this place called City of Star Machines?" Anita asked.

"Our cities are named for the main product they grow or manufacture," Eln N'Yn responded.

"City of Star Machines is where our space hardware foundry is located," Mok N'Ghai added. He clicked his mandibles together angrily and Tom guessed that the subject of the captured city was a sensitive one.

"The Chutans captured it about five months ago," Mok N'Ghai continued. "Since then, other manufacturing districts have tried hard to supply our fleet with replacement parts, but they have been of inferior quality!"

"If the Chutans hold the foundry, why don't they build their own fleet and repair the ships they have?" Anita asked.

"They do not have the technology," Mok N'Ghai replied.

"Then how—?" the young inventor caught himself, but not in time.

"You were going to ask how the Chutans are managing to make this war drag out so long, weren't you?" the princess said quietly.

"Your Highness!" Mok N'Ghai exclaimed.

"Commander, just because the answer is an embarrassment to us, the humans deserve to know the facts. They have brought an element of unpredictability into this war that has been sorely lacking in our strategy!"

Eln N'Yn looked directly at Tom and Anita. "We Skree are strong on tradition. It is our overpowering trait to do many things the way they have been done for thousands of years. The

Chutans have taken advantage of this to keep the war going. They know that it will eventually drain our resources. Their savage instincts have made it possible for them to steal many ships from us. They have conquered and enslaved other planets with them. That way they can constantly resupply their war effort."

"They must be stopped!" Anita cried out.

Eln N'Yn nodded. "I think there is a way to end the war if we can just get the foundry out of Chutan hands!" She straightened her shoulders. "You didn't ask me what First City means, so I'll tell you. Our product is government. All other city officials come there to learn the art of diplomacy. A more accurate translation might be City of Cities."

"The royal line of First City is considered to be the foundation of our culture," Mok N'Ghai explained. "Every city's royal family can trace its ancestry to it."

He paused for a moment, then went on, "City of Star Machines had five thousand inhabitants. Fortunately, the queen and most of the clans escaped. But some individuals did not. They were put in prison for refusing to work the foundry for the Chutans. Now they are all dying. We Skree cannot live without our rigid social structure. A city with no queen is a dead city. A clan with no leader is a dead clan."

He pointed sadly at the city in front of them, now aglow with its own lights and rimmed by a hazy corona that was gradually fading into the darkness of the night sky.

"Aristotle mentioned something about that," Tom said. He suddenly realized something that he felt he should have known before. The princess would soon be the queen of First City and it was the foundation of the Skree empire. If anything happened to her, the entire civilization would topple!

Dusk had fallen. The group was so engrossed in their conversation that they paid little attention to what was going on around them. Suddenly Anita's eyes widened and she stiffened.

"What's wrong?" Tom asked. Then he saw it, too!

A Chutan patrol had emerged from behind the rocks and was now surrounding them like silent shadows. Laser guns were pointed ominously at the group and both the humans and the Skree realized immediately that resistance would result in instant death. They surrendered quickly, looking at each other in hopeless desperation!

Chapter Fourteen

The captives were marched into the city by the Chutans who laughed, talked loudly, and played games along the way. Tom thought the patrol, rather than acting like a military unit, was behaving as if it was on its way to a birthday party.

"Yuck!" Anita said in a disgusted voice as they crossed the pitted surface of the spaceport. "This place looks like it was bombed. I thought the Skree had never raided this city."

"We haven't," Mok N'Ghai answered.

"Then what's going on?" Tom asked. "I'm surprised anything can land on this field—and it's filthy as well," he added, almost tripping on some garbage.

"It's the Chutans," the princess explained. "They are incapable of caring for anything."

Tom was appalled at the junkyard appearance of the field and the ships on it. He had a hunch that some of them were not even operational. He chuckled softly as he remembered how the two Chutans aboard the *Exedra* had reacted to the ship's alarm. Now he knew why they had been so frightened. He wondered how many stolen Skree ships had blown up after their sirens had screamed into the ears of Chutan crews.

Tom spotted quick glimpses of small, furry beings who darted in and out of the ships with tools in their hands, chattering wildly to each other. They were dirty and their fur was streaked and matted with a heavy black grease.

He asked one of the patrol what they were.

The Chutan looked at him in disgust and spat, "Chimmies."

Tom could not picture those noisy creatures as being the allies Maris Nim had boasted about. They hardly seemed capable of having built the jamming device for the Skree perimeter defense!

He had no further time to speculate on the Chimmies, however, as the prisoners were led through a large, open building that was as poorly maintained as the spaceport. The place looked as if it had not been cleaned for months!

The young inventor felt very vulnerable moving down a deserted hallway that was strewn with refuse as though a New Year's Eve party had passed through. City of Star Machines was virtually a ghost city and yet he had the peculiar feeling that they were being watched.

He looked over at his friends. Mok N'Ghai and the princess had not spoken a word since the capture. Anita, too, had been silent, though she seemed unusually jumpy to Tom ever since they had entered the building. He started to ask her why, but she stopped him with a quick look of warning.

A crowd of Chimmies came abruptly around a corner and headed straight for the patrol. Tom was amused to find out that somewhere in this galaxy a planet existed whose inhabitants talked all at once and still managed to survive.

The Chimmies were just as dirty and greasy as the ones who had been working on the ships, and the Chutan guards made no attempt to hide their revulsion toward the little aliens who either did not notice or did not care. No break occurred in their non-stop chattering and none of them moved over to let the Chutans and their prisoners pass.

The guards shouted at them to step aside, but the small, furry creatures ignored the order.

Strangely enough, the Chutans seemed confused and for a moment, did not seem to know what to do. One pointed his laser gun at the Chimmies, but did not fire. Tom wondered if there was a Chutan taboo about killing their allies.

Out of the corner of his eye, he saw that Mok N'Ghai had stepped in front of the princess, using his body to shield her from possible danger. Tom drifted toward them.

"I do not know what is about to happen, but I sense trouble," the Skree commander said. Tom looked around for Anita.

She was gone!

He felt a momentary stab of fear, but it was quickly replaced by hope. The beautiful redhead had apparently found a means of escape!

All at once, the Chutan guards found themselves surrounded by gibbering Chimmies. Not only surrounded, but enveloped, smothered, and otherwise rendered helpless by the mob of greasy little aliens. Tom silently cheered the Chimmies' team effort. The Chutans tried to break free, but as soon as one Chimmie was brushed aside, two others would take his place.

One of the guards lost his laser to three Chimmies. Tom saw the weapon disappear into their midst and a few moments later emerge in pieces. Three Chimmies seemed to be having an absorbing technical discussion about the parts as they were passed rapidly from hand to hand.

"This is where we cut out," Tom said to Mok N'Ghai and the princess, but before he could take a step the young inventor felt himself grabbed from behind. A hand closed over his mouth and he was dragged backwards.

Tom realized that he was being pulled toward a panel in the wall to his right that was slightly ajar. Mok N'Ghai and the princess had also broken loose from the mob and were running along with him.

"Follow me!" whispered the familiar voice of Kate One Star as she took her hand from Tom's mouth.

"Oh, Kate, am I glad to see you!" Tom whispered back as he hurried with her toward the opening.

One thing he certainly hadn't expected to find in a Skree city was a false wall panel, and the fact that their friends were free came as an even greater surprise.

When he reached the panel, he ducked through it, followed closely by Kate and the two Skree. Seconds later he heard the panel *whoosh* shut behind him. He looked around trying to find out where he was.

Then he spotted Ben and Anita. They grinned at him triumphantly.

"The whole city is honeycombed with service corridors like this one," Ben said, gesturing proudly at the maze of pipes, ducts, and wiring on both walls and the ceiling.

From the other side of the panel, Tom and his friends heard the muffled sounds of running feet and Chutans shouting at one another.

"We'd better move," Kate said. "There'll be time enough for happy reunions later." She looked at Mok N'Ghai and Eln N'Yn uncertainly.

"The Skree are now convinced that we're not on the side of the Chutans and on the right side of this war!" Tom explained.

Kate seemed satisfied and led the group through the service corridor.

"Where is Aristotle?" the young inventor asked anxiously.

"Safe and having the time of his life. You'll see," replied Ben. "Can you believe that the Chutans don't know these corridors exist?" he added. "They think the city runs by magic!"

As they trotted down the corridor, Tom quickly related to Ben and Kate the incident with the Chutans on the *Exedra.* "I've been thinking about that quite a bit and I have a theory that may help the Skree end the war," he said. "Like the Skree, we have lived with machinery for many generations. We know that moving parts need constant lubrication and that they wear out."

He paused for a moment, then went on. "If nobody takes care of things, they will soon stop functioning properly and break down, right?"

"Right. But that's a pretty advanced idea," Anita said. "It follows building the machines and being familiar with their construction. If I were from a society that had only horse-drawn plows and I were confronted with a computer-controlled interstellar spaceship, I wouldn't have any idea how to take care of it, either."

Tom nodded. "Now take that one step further. If your culture had only developed to the point of the horse-drawn plow, you would be used to having nature supply almost everything. When you run out, you just get more. Repairing a saddle that is rotting from age is a waste of time."

"Are you saying the Chutans are from a society still in its throwaway stage?" Ben asked.

"Yes," Tom said.

"That is a very accurate description of the Chutan culture," Mok N'Ghai spoke up. "Our greatest mistake was to try and help them by pushing them into an industrial society prematurely. We thought that we could alleviate some of their problems and suffering with our technology. Instead, we created chaos because they were not ready for that kind of advanced thinking."

Kate sighed. "When we were brought into the city, I saw a guard having trouble with his laser weapon. He yelled at it, called it all kinds of names, kicked it, and then walked away, I suppose, to find another one. What a waste!"

"That's the reason why the Chutans tolerate the Chimmies," Ben explained. "Those little guys have the most amazing mechanical aptitude I've ever seen! They can fix anything they get their hands on and they learn very fast. I'd put a Chimmy up against the best engineer from Swift Enterprises any day!"

Tom chuckled. "Before you do that, tell me where we're going. And where is Aristotle?"

"In the communications center," Kate replied. "He's been tapping into all the Chutans' communications through the maintenance panels. We now know how many ships the Chutans have, where they're docked, and how many are spaceworthy."

"Great!" Tom replied. "But tell me, how did you find us?"

"Aristotle picked up a strong signal from your

T-T units as soon as you came into the city," Ben said. "He also monitored the signal from the homing device in Anita's artificial leg."

"I'd forgotten all about that!" exclaimed Anita. "It was put in so that Aristotle would know our location way back when we went to visit David Luna! I'm amazed it's still working! Anyway, I started scanning for familiar emotion patterns when we arrived here. I picked up Kate and Ben, but kept losing the contacts. Maybe there are some solid objects that block my empathic sense," Anita added thoughtfully.

"That's possible," Ben said. Then he grinned. "We also know what time the base commander, Colonel Wapchis, goes to bed and how he likes his autocook device to prepare his steaks—when it's working, that is."

"The food machines are broken down?" Tom asked excitedly.

"Yep," said Ben. "It's becoming a real problem because the Chutans' supply lines are so long—several million miles, to be exact. They're worried that they won't be able to hold City of Star Machines if the Chimmies can't fix the autocook devices."

"There's an old military saying that an army travels on its stomach," Kate added. "The Chutans will soon have two choices of action. They either have to go home or attack the Skree with everything they've got. In view of their past behavior, I think they'll attack."

"We must warn the other Skree cities," said Eln N'Yn, breaking her long silence.

"We would know a lot more about their plans if we could read the symbols on things," Ben said, "but Aristotle's information bank is incomplete on the written Skree language and we've been guessing."

"We will help you in any way we can," offered Mok N'Ghai.

"If we can convince the Chimmies to help us, we can make it impossible for the Chutans to attack," Tom said eagerly. "But they don't seem to communicate with other beings and that's going to be a problem."

To the young inventor's surprise, Ben laughed. "When we get to our base you can ask the head Chimmie himself about that!"

"What?" Tom asked, puzzled.

"You'll see," said Ben. "Right around that corner!"

Tom walked forward several feet, then stopped, staring with his mouth wide open.

Chapter Fifteen

Tom's first impression of the communications center was that of a city turned inside out. It was a huge room with a barren floor. All four walls were filled with thick bundles of wiring which ran into bulk-connectors at random intervals. The ends of the wires disappeared into the backs of giant machine panels.

"My circuits are once again functioning at their peak efficiency!" said Aristotle, looking up from the group of Chimmies sitting in front of him like children hearing a story.

Evidently puzzled, Mok N'Ghai stared directly at Tom.

"That's Aristotle's way of saying he's glad to see me," Tom said.

"You have a very sophisticated mechanoid," the Skree commander admitted. "We experimented with such robots at one time but soon found that they tended to destroy our peace of mind more than they served us."

"I know what you mean," the young inventor whispered with a grin.

"I was just reciting the chassis repair manual for the Swift Enterprises' N-445 Light-duty Shuttle," Aristotle said. "They will be annoyed with me for leaving them in the middle of the chapter on component replacement for the fusion-drive initiator."

"How did you ever get away from the Chutans?" Tom asked.

"The Chimmies are true connoisseurs of the machine arts," the robot explained. "So naturally when they first saw me, it awakened their inherent deep appreciation of form and beauty."

Ben laughed. "In other words, it was love at first sight. Within minutes after we entered the city, we were mobbed by hundreds of Chimmies. They were all over Aristotle and when the guards tried to pull them away, the Chimmies got mad. It was a little frightening. Anyway, the Chimmies were afraid that the Chutans would disassemble Aristotle and they decided to save him and us—although they would have left Kate and me to the Chutans if Aristotle hadn't made a big fuss about that. We're only acceptable because we're his friends," Ben explained.

"I'm surprised there were no reprisals against the Chimmies," said Anita. "Surely the Chutans will punish them for helping us get away."

"I doubt it," said Kate. "They need the Chimmies. Besides, they would have to punish all of them just to get the guilty ones because they can't tell them apart."

"We've got to do something to prevent the Chutans from launching a full-scale attack on the Skree," Tom said. He furrowed his brow with deep concentration and began pacing. The Chimmies looked at Aristotle, unsure of what to think of his tall blond human friend.

"We have to launch an attack of our own. That's what we have to do!" the young inventor muttered. "We have to hit them at their most vulnerable point and start them running. Right now they're hungry and getting hungrier by the minute. That'll make them desperate and a desperate opponent doesn't think rationally. We'll hit them with the only weapon we have they have no defense against—sabotage!"

"And just how do you propose to do that?" Kate asked. "We're a bunch of unarmed civilians. They're a well-armed military force!"

Tom stopped pacing and grinned at his friends. Reaching into the pockets of his jumpsuit, he brought out the silverware, the matches, and the paring knife.

Ben laughed. "Wow! We're armed with some flatware and the deadliest weapon in the galaxy—Tom Swift, genius and inventor!"

"Who's crazy!" Kate added.

"Trust me," Tom said. "I have a plan and if it works, the Chutans will run for home—and stay there!"

He whispered to Aristotle for a moment, then waited while the robot passed on some instructions to the Chimmies. A group of the furry creatures immediately ran to uncap an opening, then stood back, chattering, to see what would happen next.

Tom simply dropped a fork—one-third of his flatware collection—into the hole.

There was an instant flash and bits of charred, half-melted silver exploded from the access hole. All the lights in that section of the city went out.

Aristotle turned on one of his built-in worklights and said, "That was crude but effective."

Out of the corner of his eye, Tom saw Eln

N'Yn turn her face away. He wondered if the Skree were capable of tears.

"I'm sorry, Your Highness," the young inventor said softly. "Sometimes it's necessary to make sacrifices. I hate destroying this beautiful city, but—"

"It is expedient," Mok N'Ghai finished for him. "I learned the meaning of the word sacrifice early in my military career. I've never liked the sound of it, though. It describes a cold act that belies the deep sorrow felt by those who have to make it so that many will benefit."

"I thought that rescuing the humans and their robot would be an exciting adventure," said the princess. "Now I am filled with a great sadness. I no longer feel like a child. A city must die to save a world and that is a heavy weight to bear. City of Star Machines is not just a hollow shell of rock and metal and glass. It is a living thing. It carries the life force of the Skree that built it. I mourn its death just as I would mourn the death of any living being."

"Maybe we will be able to repair the damage," the Skree commander said in a comforting tone.

"Perhaps we can help you," Kate offered. "But tell us, Tom, what do we do now?"

"First we shake up the Chutans. Get them off

center and nervous by making the city fall apart around them. They think it runs by magic so they'll be scared to death when things start breaking down. Then we get them out of here," said Tom.

The young inventor held up a knife and spoon. "I still have these left. Come on!" He pointed out a dimly lit exit and Aristotle's light guided them.

In another basement, they put the spoon across a terminal and another section of the city went powerless. The knife was used two blocks away, dropped into the mechanical maw of a gearing device which controlled the huge antenna that searched the sky for incoming ships.

Ben caught up to them, led by a squad of chattering Chimmies. "I set fire to a stack of wood, which burned the insulation off the power line between the perimeter alarms and their independent power supply, and it shorted out. We can go anywhere now and the Chutans won't know."

"Good!" Tom said.

The noise of the Chimmies' talk was beginning to hurt his ears, but he could hardly blame the little aliens for being excited. They were taking apart an entire city! Still, it was so loud that he could hardly think. "Will you take them somewhere and keep them quiet?" he shouted to Aristotle.

"They are only exchanging technical information," the robot said.

"And I can't hear. You go tell them what we planned and get them to spread the word," Tom said.

"Yes, Tom." The robot left, wading along in a bouncing, hip-high pool of noisy Chimmies.

Tom looked at his watch. "Let's synchronize our time. I have twenty-one hundred and twenty seconds *now!*"

Kate, Anita, and Ben adjusted their watches for the fractional differences.

Tom glanced at the two Skree and frowned. Then he took off his wristwatch and handed it to Mok N'Ghai. "You'll need this more than I will," he declared.

"Thank you," the commander said.

"Now we get to phase two," Tom went on. "Each of you will have a job to do. But remember, you only have one chance. If you fail, we've had it!"

He discussed his plan with his friends and the Skree, then watched them run through the maintenance passages, going in different directions. When they were out of sight, he ducked around the corner, slipped under some dripping pipes, and hurried through the underground spaceport.

He had kept the biggest job for himself—to sabotage the entire spacefleet!

Chapter Sixteen

It was dark when Tom cautiously emerged from the service tunnel. The spaceport stretched out miles long before him, a concrete plain blotched by fiery jets and populated with Chutan ships.

He counted nine Skree vessels—the booty of a war that should not have happened. Tom found the one described to him as the flagship of the stolen fleet.

He crept across the launch surface toward the flagship, avoiding the brighter patches of light from the unsabotaged buildings and worklights.

There was a guard but he never knew what hit him when Tom karate-chopped him between his helmet and battle armor. The boy dragged the unconscious Chutan into a hiding place between some supplies, then quickly went up the ladder into the main airlock.

Inside, Tom stopped, listening for sounds, but all he heard was the soft whisper of the air-conditioning and the tiny flicks of automatic devices at work.

All was normal. Or so it seemed to be.

Tom headed for the level just below the control deck where all the computer equipment was installed. He needed one specific terminal and one specific code word.

He knew the word—the Skree word for starlight—and he found the terminal. He studied it for several minutes, anxious not to make any mistakes.

Then his fingers began tapping out the word, releasing the lock on the terminal. Now he had access to the ship's master computer, and that electronic brain had every other Chutan ship connected to it through their computer.

Tom began to slowly construct the program as he worked with the unfamiliar keys in a language he had to fumble through.

Suddenly the alarms went off!

Bells began to ring all over City of Star Machines. Sirens whined. Buzzers sounded. Screens lit up with MALFUNCTION signs. Emergency doors slammed shut.

Eeeeeeeeee!

Whang! Whang! Whang! Whang!

EEEEeeeeeEEEEEeeeeEEEEEeeeeEEEEeeee!

Bzp! Bzp! Bzp!

MALFUNCTION. MALFUNCTION.

Borp! Borp!

Beep! Beep! Beep! Beep!

"This is Automatic Emergency Control. Switch to emergency channels only! ADX-17s will report to their posts! This is Automatic Emergency Cont—"

BONG! BONG! BONG!

Tom ignored the clamoring from the alarms and finished the program. Then he took a deep breath. He could only hope he had made no mistakes because there was no time to check.

The young inventor jumped up, switching on a screen for an exterior view. Chutans were running out of the city in droves!

Tom scrambled down the ladder when he heard the lock mechanism cycling.

Someone was coming in!

He ducked into a tiny officer's cabin right next to the lock and huddled behind the computer terminal. He reached up and switched on a monitor, directing the computer to choose a view from the cameras facing the city.

The Chutans were running for their ships. Something exploded and flames reflected off a slim golden spire. Tom was hoping that Mok N'Ghai and the princess were being careful with the explosives. The charges had to be timed just right.

The airlock opened.

A stocky Chutan ran in with a frightened look on his face. Tom was relieved to discover the savage alien didn't smile. Another Chutan rushed in and shoved the first one aside. He looked frightened, too, but also seemed capable of rational action.

"Prepare for takeoff!" he shouted.

"But Colonel Wapchis," the first Chutan wailed in panic, "what if the magic that destroyed the city has touched the ships as well?"

The colonel didn't answer. Instead, he stood stock-still, listening.

Tom grabbed his T-T unit and switched it off. He had grown so accustomed to it that he had forgotten about it. But the colonel, having heard the soft tones of the translator speaking in a language he did not understand, knew something was wrong!

The Chutan yelled out some angry sounds that Tom couldn't understand without the T-T unit.

The young inventor froze and tried to make himself invisible. He listened to the movements of the excited Chutans who were looking for him.

Seconds later he felt the tip of a laser pistol pressed against his temple. Knowing it was all over, he switched the unit back on in mid-tirade.

"—you think you're doing, you—" Colonel Wapchis jumped back, almost firing as he heard the strange language once more. "What kind of being are you that can double-speak?" he asked, an edge of fear in his voice.

"It's my translator," Tom said quickly.

"Of course," said the colonel. Tom could tell that the alien was not convinced. "Do not disappear this time or I will shoot!" Wapchis shouted. "Where is your ship?"

"Disappear?" Tom asked. Then he realized that the Chutan was referring to his escape into the service corridors. The young inventor decided not to give the secret away. Let the alien think it was part of the magic. "The ship is not here," Tom said. "And you can't steal it!"

"No matter," said the colonel. His smile had returned and he waved the laser in Tom's face. "I have you. You can build all of the lightning ships I want! Then the Chutans will defeat the bugs!" He spat.

"Colonel!" The guard that Tom had clobbered was staggering into the lock, his knees weak, his voice only a croak. "Colonel, they're—" His eyes rolled up and he collapsed, striking his head sharply on the deck.

The colonel looked at him for a split-second, then swung his gun back at Tom, his face a mask of anger. But Tom had moved quickly. His hand lashed out, striking at the colonel's laser. The weapon flared once, burning into the deck before a second blow from Tom knocked it from the Chutan's fist, and his well-placed punch sent the commander flying backward.

The young inventor scooped up the laser, then scrambled out of the airlock. Another explosion, this one close to the edge of the spaceport, brightened the whole evening sky. Tom jumped, hitting the ground in a roll, and was zigzagging away from the flagship as Colonel Wapchis cursed him from the airlock.

A ship's drive ignited and it rose slowly into the night sky, the intense glare from its flaming tail putting everything into stark relief.

Dropping behind a plastic packing crate, Tom surveyed the field. Another fighter was beginning to rise. Chimmies were being herded aboard one ship at gunpoint. The gun disappeared from the Chutan's grip and came apart in the mob of chittering creatures almost at once. Then they simply walked away, passing the pieces of the weapon back and forth.

Frustrated, the guard scrambled up the ladder to the airlock. He had barely entered the ship when the takeoff alarm sounded. Seconds later the craft lifted.

Three. Four. Five and Six lifted at once. Seven.

The flagship spat fire and left a seared circle on the pitted surface of the spaceport.

Then the last ship took off, far down at the end of the field.

The Chutans were gone!

Tom rose and stretched. A group of Chimmies came out of the darkness and took apart a small electric cart on their way toward him. One of them unzipped Tom's wristband and put his hairy arm searching up his sleeve before Tom slapped his arm. "Hey! Stop that! What are you doing?" he yelled.

Ben, Anita, and Kate came trotting out of the darkness. They were grinning in delight and telling each other what a wonderful thing it was to see the Chutans leave. The grins faded, however, when they noticed Tom looking beyond them with great sadness in his eyes. All turned to see City of Star Machines enveloped in flames!

"Where are Eln N'Yn and Commander N'Ghai?" Anita asked suddenly, glancing around the spaceport in desperation.

"They were going to bring out any Skree prisoners that might have been held by the Chutans," Kate explained. "I guess they didn't make it." Her voice broke when two figures suddenly emerged from the flaming inferno!

The princess and the commander ran toward them, enveloped in what looked like wet blankets. They appeared unhurt.

Tom breathed a sigh of relief. At the same time, he felt deeply saddened. Obviously there were no other survivors. "One city had to die tonight," he said slowly, "so that many others can live."

Aristotle waded toward him, surrounded by a hundred Chimmies. More were coming from every direction. But Tom's almost indestructable mechanoid was missing his left arm!

"Aristotle! What happened?" he shouted. The question was answered a split-second later when the pieces were being passed through the crowd of Chimmies. "What have you started, Aristotle?" said the young inventor, annoyed. "Tell them to put your arm back!"

"They are merely curious. They would not hurt me. I thought you would appreciate their curiosity and that you would not mind if I—"

"Tell them!" Tom insisted.

"Yes, Tom." Aristotle chittered away for a moment and even Tom's T-T unit blipped and squawked as it missed words. In a moment, the arm came floating through the crowd, passing from hand to hand. Several Chimmies swarmed atop the robot and the arm was attached again. Aristotle flexed it and chittered something at the tiny brown, furry aliens. They chittered back.

"I believe they have improved its fluidity, Tom," Aristotle said with a note of pride in his voice. "I have been trying to coach them in sophisticated techniques and it seems that they are deserving proteges."

"They've one-upped you," Ben grinned at Tom.

Mok N'Ghai and the princess turned to the young inventor. "Your plan was more successful than we had hoped, although the city was destroyed. You humans are a remarkable group. You have accomplished a task that no Skree would have even dreamed possible!" she said.

"With the help of the Chimmies," Anita said. "Weren't they wonderful? They sabotaged the whole place, then set off all the alarms, even patched into the command link of the ships to send *them* into space!"

Everyone looked up. The fiery trails were just distant pinpoints now.

Ben asked Tom, "What about your mission? Did you get it done?"

"I sure did. The flagship will broadcast the program to every other craft, not just the fleet that was here, but anything else the Chutans have that's within the flagship's range. They won't even know it's happening. They'd have to blow up the flagship right now to stop it!" he said.

"And when they land on their home planet—" Kate snapped her fingers and laughed.

"The ships shut down, overload their circuits, and turn to slag," Anita said gleefully.

"The Chutans will be stranded on their own planet," Mok N'Ghai cried gleefully.

"Maybe they will be better neighbors by the time they learn to build their own ships," Eln N'Yn ventured.

"Well, I guess—" Tom started, then stared in surprise at Aristotle. Now the robot's right arm was missing!

"They are fixing it," the mechanoid said apologetically. "They also told me that they would like to go work with the Skree since they have a much more advanced technology than the Chutans. The Chimmies like that."

"How about that?" Ben said to Mok N'Ghai.

The commander shrugged, his alien face assuming an expression the humans were learning meant resignation to fate. "Could we stop them, even if we wanted to?"

"Probably not." Tom laughed. "Aristotle, will you—" he stopped again. Aristotle had a new right arm.

It was twice as long as the old one!

"They are trying out something," Aristotle said. "But they'll put it back the way it was."

"You hope," Kate One Star said.

When the robot didn't respond, they all laughed. "For once, he's not so sure!" Tom said.

The farewells from the Skree were brief but emotional.

"I cannot go back to Earth with you, although I would like to," the princess said, "so I am doing the next best thing. I am sending my personal envoy, Commander Mok N'Ghai with you. He will be my eyes and ears and a fitting representative of the Skree people. I hope he can adjust to being an ordinary passenger!"

What would returning to Earth be like after all they had experienced in outer space? Tom wondered. They certainly had a lot to explain about their abrupt departure.

He also wondered about Mok N'Ghai. How would the Earth people react to him?

The young inventor looked out of the port at the galaxy of stars above. Anita and Ben followed his gaze.

"You think we'll ever have such an adventure again?" Ben asked.

Little did the friends realize what was in store for them in *Tom Swift: The Space Fortress.*